Praise for Earl S. Braggs' previous work:

What is and has always been needed is an honest, clear, loving voice. Earl Braggs' *Ugly Love (Notes from the Negro Side of the Moon)* offers that. Pull up your favorite chair and cover your cold feet with your grandmother's quilt and enjoy this wonderful read.

—Nikki Giovanni

For a long time, I have not read such a passionately and gracefully written book of poetry as Earl S. Braggs' *House on Fontanka*. Being an African American, he so deeply understands the suffering of Russia, as Pushkin's grandson, inheriting Pushkin's great gift of global compassion.... There is no guilt.

—Yevgeny Yevtushenko

Like Whitman, Braggs finds occasions for song everywhere. It is a rich, finely textured world full of surprises and insights.

—James Tate

... jaunty, heart-broken, fast-talking, and true.

—William Matthews

The reader is returned, through repetition's felicities—the epic extension of the moment of composition—inward to our national soul.

—Alice Notley

Earl S. Braggs' *Crossing Tecumseh Street* is lively, vocal, and laced with an intelligent sense of humor. I enjoyed these poems.

—Billy Collins

For this writer, form comes from the outside in ... strong stuff that matters, not the usual thing.

—Marvin Bell

Braggs powerfully bears testimony of the country's disenfranchised in rolling headlong cadences that aspire to the incantatory. They also register leaping exuberance, joy, spiritual yearning, and the majesty of enduring.

—Lynda Hull

No romanticism here, but a witnessing with wit and irony, with subtle wisdom that rises only out of the fire.

—Christopher Buckley

Powered by an incantatory rhythm in the tradition of Whitman, Braggs takes us ... into a world of dazzling visions, enormous disappointment and guarded hope.

—Richard Jackson

Morning Edge of Midnight
& After Allyson

Also by Earl Braggs

Obama's Children
Boy Named Boy, a Memoir
Cruising Weather Wind Blue
Hat Dancing Blue with Miss Bessie Smith
Negro Side of the Moon
Ugly Love (Notes from the Negro Side of the Moon)
Oliver's Breakfast in America
Syntactical Arrangements of a Twisited Wind
Younger Than Neil
In Which Language Do I Keep Silent
Crossing Tecumseh Street
House on Fontanka
Walking Back from Woodstock
Hat Dancer Blue
Hats

Morning Edge of Midnight & After Allyson

Short Stories

Earl S. Braggs

Lake Dallas, Texas

Printed in the United States of America

FIRST EDITION

Permissions
Madville Publishing
PO Box 358
Lake Dallas, TX 75065

Cover Design: Jacqueline Davis

ISBN: 978-1-963695-47-2 paperback,
978-1-963695-48-9 ebook

Library of Congress Control Number: 2025946847

For my wife, Natalie Strelnikova Braggs

Table of Contents

Howard and Hannah

(Back to the World)

There was, literally, nothing left to be said about how love travels in mysterious directions. The end of their opening monologues corresponded with the "Thank you, Jesus" sounds of landing gear touching down on runway number 17, LAX. For 18 hours and some change, the voices of their small-town stories had no reason to stop talking. For the duration of the flight, they did not fall asleep beyond a few Southeast Asian cat naps taken on the thin and broad shoulders of comfort and availability. By the longest stretch of a stretched to the limit imagination, an 18-hour flight from Vietnam to the US (Back to the World) was not enough time for two strangers to fall, so evenly, in love. But somehow, 1970 became 1971 overnight that night on that flight.

Hannah grew up in a California trailer park community outside of Truckee. Some years, tying strings together to make ends meet, Hannah's parents got the pieces to fit. Other years, they were just hard-working poor folks, coming up short. Hannah doesn't remember ever going to church, though her parents told her that they used to take her. Her extended family all lived in Salt Lake City or Provo, Utah. Hannah and her mother and father lived in Donner Creek Mobile Home Park. Playground years and teenage years in a place named after the 1847 fate of the Donner Party haunted Hannah. It was little wonder that

Hannah wanted to get away from her hometown trailer park notoriety. Day-to-day trailer-park life for Hannah was escaping the day-to-day part. She was on the basketball team in junior high, but her dribbling talent didn't transfer. In high school she was a bench warmer on the softball team. Her claim to high school fame was that Hannah was number 3 on the tennis team her junior and senior years. She was gone from home all the time. Many days, she stayed after school and went to practice even when there was no practice. She took up residence in the Truckee Public Library to the point that some Saturdays she would not have been surprised if Miss Sadie or one of the other librarians had asked for rent money. Southern literature was an escape. She loved stories set in the South. She always realized why she identified so easily with the climate, the culture, the staging, the neuroticism of stories set in the South, but she never shared why with anyone until she met Howard. She rarely saw anybody she knew at the library; she didn't want to. But there was this Black boy about her age that seemed to always be there on Saturdays. "Was he in his corner?" was the first thing that entered Hannah's mind every Saturday during her senior year. She loved his dark profile. He had an actor's face. He never took the time to look her way. Sometimes, Hannah would get close enough to see what he was reading, and it always appeared to be a play, an easy guess since he looked so theatrical. His quiet stage presence, Hannah thought she loved, but she could never bring herself to say hello. One day as he was leaving, she noticed that he did look without looking directly at her. She paid careful attention to the book he placed back on the shelf, *Mormons in Paris*: Polygamy on the French Stage, 1874-1892. Maybe it was a message, maybe not. Hannah thought but was afraid to believe.

The tragic fate of the Donner Party included several large Mormon families. Why would they name a trailer park after a tragedy? Hannah could never bring herself to ask her parents that question or the other question. Among her high school friends, none lived the Donner Trailer Park lifestyle. Most of the trailer-park kids Hannah grew up with went to the neighborhood high school. Hannah's mother worked as a secretary in a law firm. The senior partner helped Hannah get a four-year scholarship to an all-important private high school, literally, one mile away from Hannah's home. Though she took the city bus to and from school, Hannah counted all 5,280 feet on a weekly basis. She loved walking, especially in the rain. Because the private school required uniforms, no one could tell what styles and latest trends in fashion Hannah couldn't afford to wear. Hannah's high school dating life was a puzzle with odd shaped, non-fitting pieces. Sometimes her high school dating life was a crossword of rich boys coming to her trailer-park house to pick her up, rich boys dropping her off at her trailer-park house, rich boys asking for a kiss and more, but not asking for a second date. Hannah was the prettiest "girl next door" of the bunch, but among her close girlfriends, she was the only one who did not "go steady" at one time or another. The lot of them were private school, drive-in picture show girls. Hannah saw every drive-in movie worth seeing, especially those that debuted on '64 and '65 California summer nights. College movie night was the higher education side of the same story with an angled ending that ended pretty much the same. She dated several nice fellows, and several nice fellows wanted more time than she was ready to give in exchange for their being nice fellows. So, she gave in to the slow speed of love and took a "slow boat" to the South China Sea and ended up in Vietnam. December 29th, 1969 was one of the last days of the Year of the Rooster and Hannah was tired of listening to the fades of fate. Though she didn't go to Woodstock, Jimi Hendrix, wearing a Sagittarian blue bandana, was still playing the Star-Spangled Banner in Hannah's ear when she touched down upon dry season, Southeast Asia.

Howard grew up in the middle of a Southern literature short story plot with no missing puzzle pieces. A fishing village between two swamps, within walking distance of fresh water and salt water, the place he called home. Howard was born with his back to the ocean. All of his growing up years, he knew that all he had to do was turn around and praise the beauty of sunrise over water. Raised in the deep, southeast corner of North Carolina, he was from South Carolina as much as he was from North Carolina. Except for one other Black man and wife with no children, Howard and his grandmother were the only Black people living in Howard's fishing village during those years. All through school, Howard was the only Black student in all of his classes. There was never a hint of racism that Howard recognized as such. Howard's grandmother worked, domestically, for a lot of the white families in the community. Howard grew up playing with and going to school with their children. Although they always sat in the back pew, Howard and his grandmother attended services at the white Methodist church, and when Howard was old enough, he played center field on the church's baseball team. It was never publicly acknowledged, but Howard's first, second and third girlfriend were white. Everybody loved Howard and Howard loved his fishing village-country life. He grew up chasing deer, catching fish, trapping crabs, netting shrimp, gigging flounder, digging clams, quail hunting and finding quiet spots beneath trees to read novels, none of which he ever finished because of his undying love of short stories.

Howard's community was the first stop on the book mobile route. Howard would always check out more books than two weeks would allow him to read. Sometimes Miss Simpson, the book mobile lady as everybody called her, would let Howard ride the whole route with her. She talked about everything in the world, but the way she talked about Howard's father made Howard think that maybe the book mobile lady loved his father a little more than she loved him. Both of Howard's parents read stories to him when he was little. They decided upon separate directions when he was seven. The year his parents separated and moved as far away from Howard as they could get, he repeated second grade. Over his growing up years, each parent would visit him, especially on birthdays and holidays, but they never again made quite the same literary impression on Howard.

He was nineteen, fresh out of a two-year infatuation with a girl named Kaylyn, wearing bell bottom blue jeans and tie dye, the day he got his draft notice via US Postal Svc. Why did he check the mail that day? He was three weeks from high school graduation. Earlier that spring, the book mobile lady wrote a reference letter that got him a scholarship to attend the university in the fall, but the U. S. Army refused to recognize Howard as being worthy of a college deferment. 1969, The Summer of Love was a bootcamp summer of war for Pfc. Howard Rollins Jr.

The simultaneity of Howard and Hannah's tours of duty, 12 months to the day, ending on the same calendar day; the simultaneity of shipping out of country, 6 days later, on the same calendar day; the simultaneity of flying out of Da Nang Air Base on the same commercial flight, Pan Am Flt. 314; the simultaneity of assigned seats next to each other in the middle row was too simultaneous not to have been pre-programmed by something quicker than the speed of everything.

So, they took it as such without recognizing it as such. From the moment they settled into their seats, their carry-on luggage, placed beneath their seats, snuggled and hugged as if they were suitcase buddies with a history of traveling around the world together. She touched him for the first time when she leaned into him while trying to dislodge her seat belt from beneath her. He touched her for the first time as he was trying to buckle in for the flight Back to the World. By the time the airline stewardess said, "Your seat cushion can be used as a floatation device," they had already drowned in the deepest part of the Pacific Ocean, simultaneously.

Liftoff lifted a lot of the weight of war from their shoulders, still the weight of that undeclared war was heavy enough to carry the beginning chapters of their small-town stories. Hannah was a Second Lieutenant in the Air Force. Howard was a soul sky soldier, he jumped out of airplanes. He was a Pfc. in the 82nd Airborne Division, an elite division out of Fort Bragg, North Carolina. Fraternization between an officer and an enlisted person was an improper relationship- arrangement according to the Military Code of Justice. He was Black, beautiful and brown and she was California-pretty, a white girl. Therefore, Howard plus Hannah was the evidence of a Saturday night, Southern cross-burning crime. And so, the story of Howard and Hannah began with them trying to find balance on a slope.

The float of a smooth ride out of a rough place hypnotized them as soon as Pan Am Flt. 314 reached cruising altitude. Though they were sitting next to each other, on a day-to-day cultural level, they were flying at different altitudes. An east coast country boy, 11 time zones from home and a California girl, 14 time zones from home falling in love with the sounds of what each other's voice carries to the other. Most war-calendar days refuse to be erased. Leaving Vietnam on a jet airplane caused each of them to reflect upon the day they arrived. Howard remembers and Hannah remembers stepping down from a jet airplane into a non-blowing South China Sea breeze.

Hannah Ashtyn Christensen volunteered to serve her country. Hannah went to college, majored in Political Science, and taught at a community college for two quarters, which she hated, before joining the United States Air Force. She attended Officer Training School (OTS) at Maxwell Air Force Base in Montgomery, Alabama. There were things she liked about being in Montgomery. She loved the genteel laid-back-ness, but mostly she loved being in the city where Zelda Fitzgerald was born. She loved everything about F. Scott and Zelda and the greatness of *The Great Gatsby*. She loved all the expats and their café lifestyle of 1920s Paris. She always wanted Paris, France to be her first overseas trip, but Southeast Asia stole the show. And it wasn't a good show. It was a racing-to-survive horror movie with no end-line closing credits rolling down the screen telling the audience who produced and directed the Oscar nominated, *On the Edge of Hell.*

Any sky over any war is a Fourth of July-celebrating-sky every night. Hannah celebrated her 23rd birthday eating Vietnamese rice cake without lighting a candle. There was no need to, the sky lit up 23 candles just for Hannah that night. Vietnam wasn't all bad, though. It couldn't be, no one would be able to handle all that badness. Mail-call time was always on time, and it was always good to get a letter from home. Letters from home were, pretty much, always good news. Letters from home rarely carried bad news to a soldier. Between the five-month-in-country calendar mark and the day she got her orders Back to the World, Hannah got to go to Bangkok and Manila for R&R (Rest and Recuperation) twice. Within the ranks of war conditions and killing circumstances, those two trips were as good as it gets. Hannah, as a WAF (Women in the Air Force) spent her tour of duty in the rear, Long Binh Post, a major rear base near Saigon. She served in SAC (Strategic Air Command). As a second Lieutenant, Hannah commanded a flight of airmen that supported Operation Arc Light, a series of sustained aerial bombardment campaigns. About two months into her tour of duty, Hannah was so annoyed with being called "Hanoi Hannah," she psychoanalyzes everything from the beginning. Name-calling stopped as suddenly as it began when she refused to let it bother her anymore. Dying and dead possibilities were real, but aside from Vietcong rockets and mortars when they decided to rain down upon Da Nang, Hannah was cautiously unafraid of being zipped up in a body bag.

Out in the bush, "Gazing like Buddha as far into the future as into the past," Howard counted body bags on a weekly basis. Out in the bush, handsome laughter is terrifyingly nervous. The war sounds of yesterday, today and tomorrow disappear one marked-off-calendar-day at a time. Howard spent his tour of duty dropping from the sky into rice paddy fires and jungle clearings. Squatting in shadows, watching trees move, wearing the weight of love and war around his shoulders like the fit of a full metal jacket, he was glad it was harder to see a soul soldier in the dark. Monsoon liquids, blended mud, snakes, booby traps, "watch where you step," no need to repeat. For four to five weeks at a time, Howard's days were long patrols through dense jungles and rice paddies. Constant vigilance for ambushes and limited access to anything basic was routine. Some soldiers carried lucky coins, others carried lucky seashells. Some soldiers carried rabbit feet in their pockets for whatever luck they would bring. Some soldiers wore strange things like the soldiers who wore their girlfriend's panty hose around their necks for good luck and that sexual healing feeling. Howard carried or wore nothing. He trusted what his grandmother always told him, "You look just like your daddy, you were born lucky." Out in the bush, flame throwers and grenades created visual art, framed it before your eyes and hung still wet paintings on the walls of dead living rooms.

Howard's eyes were sharp shooters. He always volunteered to walk point. Every soldier in the platoon respected the craziness of that kind of valor. His nights were mostly hotel foxholes unless he was assigned to go out on night patrol. Booby traps and tree snipers constantly trapped each man's attention to the point that each man could see up and down without looking up or down. He could see behind himself without turning his head beyond 15 degrees. Out in the bush, they learned to read signs in the flight patterns of birds. Howard was a soul soldier; soul music was his prayer. Out in the bush, every sunrise was Thanksgiving morning. The speed and direction of wind was informative, full of warnings about how not to wake up listening to Grateful Dead music.

Row 37, 10 reddish brown alphabet seats across: Window

ABC aisle DEFG aisle HIJ Window. Situated, snugly, between seat D and seat G were Howard and Hannah's assigned seats. Seats E and F saw them boarding directly behind each other before they realized that they would be sitting next to each other. After they did the overhead bend fit-trick and claimed their assigned seats, they were still too preoccupied with parades of flashback moments to notice that seat D and seat G were still unassigned seats when Pan Am Flt. 314 slowly pushed back from gate 19. Back to the World, they were bound. "Floating Across the Sky over the Pacific in a Love Boat," the idea didn't have time to enter their minds before they were on their way. Howard and Hannah, seat-buckled in, holding onto what they did not know was there to hold on to. His first words to her fell in love with her first words to him. The tender sounds of each other's voices held tender moments together long enough for each of them to savor before swallowing the sweet aftertaste of what was said.

Dressed as glamorous images, Pan Am stewardess#1 and stewardess#2 welcomed Howard and Hannah with the congratulatory comfort reserved for couples flying off to the honey side of the moon. Howard and Hannah, side by side, in spaces defined by sideways-eye-contact. To each other, each explained and described the foreshadowing fields planted across the backdrops of their stories. Each word, happily forced to feel the facial expressions of fairy tales. Neither believed fairy tales ever came true until they looked into the eyes of themselves in make-believe mirrors on the backs of the seats directly in front of them.

Avenues of stories, streets of stories, back country roads of stories, they told each other. Each story decided to be told unedited with no reservations, no hesitations. From the moment they met, something smaller than a moment exploded into even smaller plot pieces that neither of them had ever been told. The stars in Howard's eyes, Hannah didn't even have to notice to feel the dreamy effects of his starry nights. By just being pool water blue, Hannah's eyes were happy to delight in listening to Howard's voice. Every fasten-your-seat-belt checker looked at Howard and Hannah twice, sitting side by side with no one on either side of them in a four-passenger middle row of seats. Boarding soldiers, sailors, marines, war correspondents and civilians had looked at them without looking at them. In for a long ride, Howard and Hannah were writing a musical score. The opening song of their 8-track tape compilation, to be composed by the end of the flight, was already playing Marvin Gaye, *What's Going On* by the time Pan Am Flt. 314 tucked in her landing gear.

Intro. to Religion of Love 101, a college course with no required text, could not account for the magic. 33,000 feet above ground love, what a place and time to take classroom attendance. They say time doesn't know how to stand still, but by the time the control tower cleared Pan Am Flt. 314 for take-off, something that early evening made time stop for a moment and listen to the colors of wind blowing across the runway. Complete strangers fifteen moments before they met, completely in awe of each other within the first fifteen moments after meeting. 30 seconds is a long time when counting horizonal.

Acting, reacting, exacting proportions of patience and poise for 18 hours and some change, their stories unfolded first on one side of midnight, then on the other side of midnight. For Howard and Hannah, ample space and fun times filled every hint of emptiness. They played bridge without crossing over, jumping off or walking under. They played chess without pieces, checkmating each other in castled corners by memorizing each other's moves until they moved to Paris circa 1927. *April in Paris*, les rues of spring showers and parasol umbrellas waiting for the sun. Howard and Hannah on a midnight train to Amsterdam. Howard and Hannah walking in rain all the way to Spain and back, hop-skipping between showers. For 18 hours and some change, they touched every part of each other's body with the flow of each other's words. They loved to hear themselves talk to themselves.

Slow tempo, rock steady, even the air smelled like Jazz on the streets of Marseille. Every street corner light post was Sidney Bechet blowing his soprano saxophone before switching to clarinet so smoothly, the switch couldn't be seen with the naked eye. Every City of Lights, Moulin Rouge moment measured its worth by the erotic sway of Josephine Baker hips, dancing at the Theatre des Champs-Elysees. Everywhere she looked, the popularity of American jazz made Hannah think of F. Scott, Zelda and the vibrant 1920s, liberated atmosphere of expat café society. Reflected in the eyes of who they were was who they were becoming.

For 18 hours and some change, Howard took Hannah, four times, to the most expensive restaurant on the most expensive street in Pan Am City. Like new love waiting to last forever, four times they ate from each other's plate without a single thought of whose spoon was whose spoon or what fork to use when eating seatbelt-sign , light salad. Cruising across the sky, 33,000 feet above sea level, Howard and Hannah were completely unaware that they were just 57 miles below the boundary of outer space.

Take the long way home. Their 18-hour flight was a long flight that turned out to be not long enough, even after adding 36 minutes in small change. From the moment Hannah sat down next to Howard, it was like falling from a cliff. Once you're falling, you can't turn around and fall back up to the edge of love. Howard was trained to freefall. Hannah learned quickly to trust the fall. When Hannah's eyes first met the solidness of Howard's hands, the steadiness of Howard's gaze made Hannah's heart remember beautiful things. Cabin pressure multiplied in response to airline coach layout and seating arrangement. And for a moment, the tick-down to take off time stopped ticking before resuming at the speed of their heartbeat. When two hearts beat as one, one breath breathes as two.

The world turns in mysterious ways most days. 18 hours and some change to reach an ending that never intended to be reached is magical. Howard and Hannah's stories, the voices of too many words to fit as perfectly as they did. Miracles are made to happen on purpose, butterflies only land on the shoulders of the still, some blessings are too beautiful to name, the patience of trees is a virtue. Howard and Hannah talked all night and into the next day. And when they did take Southeast Asian cat naps, they talked to each other in each other's sleep.

Soon upon arrival, somewhere over the Pacific, scattered clouds divided by a polaroid blue sky provided just enough natural light for a polaroid camera to stick its lens in through the window-seat windows on either side of Howard and Hannah's mid row seats. "Say cheese," a focused polaroid angle of view instructed with the confidence of a professional photograph maker. "Click," a single studio portrait snapped in airplane cabin natural light, fanned and air dried by airline cabin pressure and presented to Howard and Hannah by the crew of airline stewardesses as evidence of their crime and their passion. Howard and Hannah sat looking into the eyes of a polaroid of themselves, smiling in and out of focus. They were not star struck; they were amazed by the beauty of their contrast. There is no black without white, there is no left without right, there is no up without down, there is no Howard without Hannah and there is no Hannah without Howard. The speed of love is quicker than the speed of light, they were so in awe, they didn't hear the pilot announce, "We have just begun our initial descent."

Minutes later, the pilot tells the crew to prepare for landing, then and tells passengers to be certain seat backs are straight up and seatbelts are fastened. Stewardesses check to make sure everything is set before strapping in for touchdown, LAX. Cheers erupted to the sounds of soldiers, sailors, airmen, and marines welcoming themselves Back to the World. Taxiing to the gate was hypnotic in a wide-open conscious way, all cylinders, numb and alive. Answers and questions Howard and Hannah avoided for 18 hours and some change changed from "maybe later" to "now:" They would be in touch. How would they find a way to kiss goodbye, how would they promise each other the moon, how would they promise the stars, how would they promise planets, how would they stay in touch? They would write every day, they would call as often as possible, they would plan to meet in a couple of months and really dance in Spanish rain. They would dress up one evening soon in gown and tux and big-band-dance at the Apollo. Christmas Eve in New York City snow, how could they promise the weather? Back to the World at the end of the world, "Where would they go from here?"

Anticipating what you are not anticipating flows slow as lava, cooling. For Howard and Hannah, disembarking and the walk to Baggage Claim took longer than an 18-hour flight from over-there to over-here. By the time they made it to carousel #34, it seemed that everybody else was already there, semi circled around a dead-still carousel, waiting for signs of life to start moving. And then the sound of a bell before movement, around and around everything started to move towards and away. The conveyor belt called out the names of brilliant-colored luggage first and the named claimed themselves right out of the shoot. Then, the shapes of luggage to come is claimed more slowly. Every piece of luggage, glanced upon by every passenger. Every passenger, looking to reclaim at Baggage Claim that separated part of themselves. Stenciled names and serial numbers on duffel bags and sea bags are harder to spot. Love in times of war can be near-sighted. Howard and Hannah moved closer to the edge of the conveyor belt to see if they could see what they ultimately saw.

An on-time arrival, airline gates of reassurance waited, patiently, to receive the relieved spirits and wounded hearts aboard Pan Am Flt. 314. It's funny how a soldier misses living so close to death so quickly. There is something safe about knowing from which direction death would come, if death decided to come. Out in the bush, soldiers just sat there, waiting for something hollow to swallow the romance of war. They waited for something deep enough to disappear "death" into something nobody cares to name. Out in the bush, every soldier is always scared. Some prayed to God, some prayed to Mohammed, some prayed to neither, while others prayed to either depending on how close one gets to death before one smells it. 14 time zones away, on the other side of the world, Vietcong rice paddies, a day taller.

Nearly half of the Pan Am Baggage Claim, semi-circled audience had left the building when Hannah spotted the stenciled-in, bold black letters of her last name, spelled out as beautiful as she had ever seen them. Immediately behind, even more prominently beautiful, Howard's duffel bag name, bolder and blacker, seemed to be pushing hers, playfully, as if intended. Howard and Hannah were holding hands, fingers locked, like parting lovers when they saw that somebody or something or some something had locked her US Airforce duffel bag to his US Army duffel bag. As far as the eye could see, there was no key to be found. The key had, apparently, thrown itself off a cliff. Hannah's tears melted into a smile upon Howard's waiting lips. A yet-to-be-read attached note, inked on plain airplane paper paused for a semi-circled, already standing, standing ovation. Claps and cheers drowned out the loudspeaker announcements of foreign and domestic destinations. No one on either side of the world was surprised by what the attached note said, "Thanks for flying with us, Sincerely, Pan Am."

Morning Edge of Midnight

Ashlee Anne Parker and Hudson Rivers Oliver had not known each other for one minute more than three and a half days before they got married. If they had been paying attention to what time zone they were in, paying attention to the angle of the hotel's bedside clock, they would have exchanged vows on the evening edge of midnight instead of the morning edge of midnight. Ashlee Anne said to herself, "Who gets married in the morning?" when they woke up the next morning "Married in the Morning." "If I didn't love him so much, I would blame it on the tequila," Ashlee thought while calligraphing a marriage certificate on hotel stationery. Moments before she'd surveyed a night of nuptials as if looking in the rearview mirror of her '69 VW Bug. Then and there, she decided she needed something official to notarize.

They'd checked into the Hotel Cotton Court around 10:30 Central Standard Time. Tequila T ime, it turned out to be. Printed in letters almost too small to see, a countertop calendar across the room said June 30st. Ashlee Anne and Oliver were hungry, but they decided to wait until they decided to see if Room Service was still on the menu. "The kitchen is closed," the telephone said, "but we can bring up a charcuterie board, two wine glasses and a bottle of your choice."

Twenty to twenty-five minutes later, a handsome young man knocked, politely, on the door of room number 513. Black, shiny tuxedo shoes, black jacket, black pants, white Nehru shirt, the boy at the door appeared dressed for a formal occasion. Accordingly, Ashlee Anne decided that extended evening after midnight that he was dressed to be ordained to confer holy orders from up above the ceiling of room 513. So, Ashlee Anne ordained him to marry them with a $100.00 tip on a $35.00 bottle of wine and a $15.00 board of cheese and cold cuts. Because there was no "Here comes the bride" music to play, Ashlee Anne's walk down the aisle between two queen size beds was almost silent. She was wearing a white Hotel Cotton Court robe with classic robbery-white shoes. Oliver stood waiting at the altar, wearing the Cotton Court minister's black jacket and military issued white boxer shorts with unlaced construction boots.

Ashlee Anne Parker and Hudson Rivers Oliver had no vows to exchange, they had no rings to exchange, so the Cotton Court Room Service delivery boy-minister announce, "I now announce (instead of pronounce) you, man and wife." He didn't know what else to say because that's all he needed to say. So, they kissed before he said, "You may now kiss the bride." They kissed so long, the minister of the moment asked, "May I be excused now?" Ashlee Anne gave him another hundred-dollar bill and said, "Enjoy the rest of your night."

June 26th, almost three and a half days before the evening of the unplanned elope-tion, Oliver, in shallow contemplation, was standing, stranded on the side of the road. He was hitchhiking his way from his hometown, Wilmington, North Carolina to Anywhere, California. The early evening seemed kind enough, but it was getting dark quickly. After almost thirty-five minutes of waiting between catching-a-ride possibilities, looking out from the seams of daylight as daylight blended in between dust dark and night black dark, he was way too cow-pasture-mushroom high to place a solid Vegas bet on a "next" set of headlights. Then his luck decided it saw headlights spaced too close together peep over the hill, growing in size, slower than normal. From a mile away, Oliver could tell that the cruising car was going below radar speed. It was the last days of June 1971 and at that point in his life and that point on the map, he had only one question taken from a hitch hiker's galaxy of question marks, "Will the road across America be as kind as the evening is, but beginning not to be?"

"There is only one road, and it leads everywhere," he'd read on a storefront book cover at City Lights Bookstore the first time he found himself on the streets of San Francisco. Now, Oliver was on the road again, still smoking Buddha stick thin joints, spaced out, on his way to the moon. His Dishonorable Discharge from the 82nd Airborne Division should have been honorable according to the Military Code of Justice for White Soldiers. But it wasn't according to Oliver's color of military justice. Pvt. First Class Hudson Rivers Oliver jumped out of his share of C130s. The parachutes opened on time every time like they knew Pfc. Oliver was not afraid of the free fall. The discharge summary alluded that Pfc. Oliver played his guitar too many nights past curfew, otherwise Pfc. Oliver was a model soldier. If he had not checked NEGRO in the race box, he would still be jumping out of the sky.

As the headlights got closer to the highway, to him and to an audience of cows, "Good evening and good milk in the morning" whispered a slow, soft, hot summer breeze. A string of cows headed for the barn and the bed before the shadow of the sun completely dropped behind the western edge of a beautiful photograph. Even as the hope of stopping-headlights became taillights, the questions would not forget to pose in case a photograph was there to be taken. Then, a "suddenly" that was not sudden at all came to call upon Oliver. Running-distance beyond where he stood, taillights became brake lights and brake lights always seem to make hitchhikers smile for the camera.

He grew up running track, training how to catch a whitetail deer for dinner, so he caught up with the brake lights quicker than a whitetail. The door handle was friendly, the atmosphere was inviting, the driver was a white woman with an open look, open as a book Hudson Rivers Oliver could not put down from the moment she picked him up.

She grew up on the upper edge of privilege, sitting in her parents' garage smoking nonfiltered cigarettes and roasting pans of pot while sipping Hennesy, the good stuff, Oliver surmised immediately, almost. But anyone would have come to that conclusion, based on how deep the cab of that beetle bug car was fogged-in so privilege-ly early in the evening. The question, "How far ya goin?" answered itself. So, Oliver had no further questions.

Like a wild wind directed out of the blue, she told Oliver that she already knew his name and his history in theory, but she would like to know both out of theory. She said all of this while she was telling Oliver that her name was Ashlee spelled with two e's. The history of Ashlee Anne was laid out in the back seat and the back floorboard. Oliver was a history major until he got drafted, so he knew how to line up dates and days. She had a song on her face, and it was singing a refrain. Oliver looked deep into her lyrics long enough to know the direction of her improvision. Oliver added jazz to her rhythm and her blues.

On the far side of the back seat of Ashlee Anne's Volkswagen bug was a whole country of static looking for a frequency. Oliver's Jack Kerouac backpack and his Gibson Les Paul Limited Edition found room to fit its craved maple top on top of tie-dyed piles of secondhand emotions and memories. Everything back there in the back seat of that '69 VW fell in love with everything else back there in that back seat of that '69 VW that evening until everyone and everything fell asleep except Ashlee Anne Parker and the humming highways of being *On the Road* with Oliver.

From the very beginning, perhaps even before the very beginning, Ashlee Anne and Oliver's story was a star-studded love story that could only be made during the soul-saving, hey days of Hollywood. As an early Sunday morning movie replaying a Saturday night fever, they met. They saved each other's soul music. She had the lyrics to their song already written down years before they met. He had the sheet music to their song, folded in his front pocket, just in time to throw his backpack into the back seat of her car.

Instrumental moonlight that early night promised, in no big hurry, the unlikely black and white and yellow variables of Ashlee Anne and Oliver's soft collision. Nobody mentioned the need to break the fall of falling in love. Their soft landing onto a bed of roses didn't even notice itself landing, softly, like landing on the moon. No gravity in a closed VW space when two talkers listened to a car radio singing to a night sky so crowded with stars, there was no room left for Ashlee Anne and Oliver not to choke on Ray Manzarek's keyboard smoke pushing Jim Morrison's voice down the highway. Ashlee Anne and Oliver had to stop at an after-midnight gas station to get a Coke to keep from choking, that night, on Jim Morrison's road-tripping lyrics:

Riders on the storm
Riders on the storm
Into this house, we're born
Into this world, we're thrown

From the beginning, silently loud nouns and sparks, indeed, did fly, but to the naked eye, neither noticed until it was too late to notice the luminosity of their chemistry. The beautiful brightness of celestial objects that night refused, repeatedly, to be diminished by the distance between the ways that led each of them in the direction of the other. Racial definitions explained along lines and laws of flawed ideology could not explain the way the world forgot how easy it was for them to fall off a mountain and into a puddle of rainwater love.

He was black like a Miles Davis's *'Round Midnight* trumpet solo, soloing in midtown Manhattan, circa 1956, a cool jazz poster child. She was white like a white night movie, circa 1923, a beautiful, smiling, silent picture show. He was 21with an U. S. Army issued gun. She was 27, unarmed for the moment out of necessity. She was upper upper-class. Her daddy owned everything in immediate proximity. Her mother was an Ivy League trophy wife. He was upper, lower middle class. His parents owned a 30-year mortgage on a tree lined street in a nice Negro neighborhood. Her social class and his social class met in the eye of a rock 'n roll storm three and a half days before graduation.

He grew up with his own Jimi Hendrix. His uncle Junior Boy taught him how to play a right-handed guitar upside down with his left hand. She grew up listening to the changing weather reports of Vivaldi's *Four Seasons*. She played piano until her piano played her into leaving it laying across the bed for another woman to play. Divorce is a hard weight to carry. They didn't have any kids, so she signed the papers, threw her copy in the trash and walked out the door, threw the front door key up onto the roof for the wind to find.

Both Ashlee Anne and Oliver were dream merchants with incurable cases of the dreamer's disease. A plotted course or an unplanned journey, to them, had the same amount of sway the way Christopher Columbus must have felt, thinking the world was flat, but not believing it because he knew it was round. Ashlee and Oliver knew if you go far enough this way, you come back from that way.

He read *Catcher in the Rye* when he was in tenth grade. He fell in love with the voice of his *Rye* teacher and the way she wore her dresses, slightly above regulation. She was born in love with books. She loved to read but she loved, even more, the way women talked in classic movies. She went to drive-in movies most of her teenage years. One night, she and two of her girlfriends entered riding in the trunk of Bad Billy's father's Oldsmobile. For her, *Bonnie and Clyde* played for free that night. The image of Miss Bonnie Parker posing with a pistol, smoking a cigar, left leg propped up on the chrome front bumper of Clyde's 1934 Ford Deluxe Sedan left an iconic impression on her.

Living in a sad town, dressing for sad dinners for three sad years of a seven-year marriage refused to forget the thrill of watching Miss Bonnie Parker turn the tide of any waterway with the way she looked when she looked from any angle into any man's mirror. Ashlee Anne Parker didn't know how to erase the significance of Miss Bonnie Parker's iconic impression and Ashlee Anne Parker had no intention of wanting to do so. Besides, they had the same last name. They were related on a spiritual level even if nothing is ever really level in love and divorce.

Ashlee Anne and Oliver, the two of them, like two map-pin-pointed locations trying to figure out where to put the "You are here" without the "You are here" realizing it was randomly put there. Rolling down the highway where places change places with other places without notice when you are not looking and when you are looking. The earring ringing in Oliver's left ear told him which direction to listen to most of the time. Ashlee Anne's bandana was too Woodstocky to give clear guidance anytime. Something, without a name, smiled upon each of them, simultaneously. The answer was there, written in black and white and yellow.

She was driving in circles until she came upon a straight road the night she picked up Oliver. A road without forks was exactly what she had always needed. Four and a half days before a hotel ceremony, she didn't see coming, she threw her husband, Mathew's gifts—a one-carat diamond wedding ring, a two-carat tennis bracelet and a no-carat gold necklace—into the high tide Atlantic Ocean and imagined sharks fighting over the descending gritter. She crossed her heart like the good girl she never figured out how to be, went back home for the last time, left an "I'm leaving you" note in the mailbox that read "Dear Mathew............................ All the Best, Ashlee." A salutation and a valediction with nothing written on the lines between. She knew a lawyer like Mathew would have no problem figuring out what that absence-minded note full of evidence left out.

Love is hard to figure out when you get out of the blue and into the grand wide openness of being *On the Road*. She, a Stray Cat Café cat on a stray cat night, ambling along in a navy-blue black '69 VW bug on a navy-blue black night. Comfortable in a comfortable seat, she took comfort in knowing that a navy-blue black '69 VW bug on a navy-blue night can't be seen from outer space.

Oliver was just back home after being dishonorably discharged. He was dismissed from active duty for telling the truth, "I just couldn't up and walk off stage before the band finished the last set of the night." The sergeants and captains were wearing government issued hearing aids, but apparently, they couldn't hear the jazz by design. The soul brothers told Oliver that if he had been a white lead guitar player in a white band, at least the musical outcome would have been different. Though Oliver knew that was the case, he never leaned into the idea of that. Oliver complicatedly said, "They didn't give me a Dishonorable Discharge, I earn it because I play like Hendrix."

Blessed up for church the evening Ashlee Anne picked him up, he was wearing blue jeans with holy holes in the knees as he walked along the holy side of highway 76. The sun was dropping as religiously red as he had ever seen it. He put his thumb out, a VW bug saw it, a VW bug stopped, he got into the front seat of a VW bug. He greeted and thanked the driver and fell in love. When that moment "immediately" became immediate, Oliver and Ashlee Anne fell into the blend of an anything-can-happen evening. Silence spoke, sincerely, to keep the moon from revealing who they, at that immediate moment, decided to be or not to be.

Like they were hauling a load of something forbidden across interstated-interracial lines, they drove all night, the next day and the next night to arrive exactly where they belonged, tangled in black and white and yellow. They took turns driving and sleeping and falling like holy water jealous of clouds and whatever else impends in the dark. Between Ashlee Anne's daylight and night soft sleep and Oliver's daylight and night soft snoring was the careful arrangement of radio songs and stories from the life and times of two only-child-in-the-family children.

He told Ashlee the story of his father, a reckless pretty boy determined to outlive each moment of the day, determined to beat the odds, a gambler's gambler. "My father drove a fish truck, drank moonshine, smoked unfiltered Camel cigarettes, womanized the best of the crop before and after marriage, died before he turned forty. Still, I loved my father. He told me he loved me every day. My father was my hero. I never needed Superman or Batman," Oliver bragged to Ashlee Anne. Oliver didn't say much about his grandmother and Ashlee Anne didn't need to hear much about her. The two of them were raised by Black matriarchs, so Ashlee Anne knew from birth more than Oliver needed to say. She smiled, almost, between Oliver's every word. Oliver made her laugh more than anyone had ever made her laugh, not because everything he said was funny, but because it was funny how every expression on Oliver's face seemed to fall into place even when it was too dark to see Oliver's face.

She told Oliver the story of how her father gave her the cash to buy a Porsche 911 S for her 5th wedding anniversary. She told him she didn't want to celebrate something that didn't make her happy. She told him that she went down to the dealership and while she wasn't paying full attention, a navy-blue black '69VW paid cash for her. "Paid cash for me, like I was a street woman," Ashlee Anne said out too loud. Then, something honest brought her to a level of understanding she'd needed for years. Until she heard Oliver's story of growing up black in America, she had never been able to bring herself to understand her appreciation of her father's wealth. When she juxtaposed it to the understanding of how years of slavery accounts for so much Southern wealth and retro antebellum prosperity, it all made sense when she crossed over and started to listen to the way Oliver's world turns.

But Oliver' real story was the story of his mother, the mother he loved beyond where stars hide in daylight. She left him to be raised by his grandmother when she disappeared one Saturday night. She took a bus from Wilmington, N.C. to the bright lights of New York City. He was eight years old. Oliver fell in love with New York City because his mother lived there, and he never stepped back from that love. Oliver's mother returned when he was sixteen. Oliver's mother was a welfare queen, and she used their home as a gambling casino , a liquor gallery and lottery center and a numbers-running track meet. Oliver told Ashlee Anne about the many nights he didn't come home until the morning side of midnight because he didn't want to fall asleep in Las Vegas or Atlantic City knowing the next day was a school day. But none of this distracted Oliver's love for New York City. Oliver loved New York City because his mother worked for a while in the Garment District just below Times Square on 42nd Street.

She told Oliver the story of how the sliding boards and swing sets of her neighborhood park determined ethnicity by measuring children's color and weight before they, mostly, disallowed swingers and sliders to swing and slide. Ashlee Anne was raised by a Black woman, Miz Lizzie. Ashlee Anne loved Miz Lizzie because Miz Lizzie loved Ashlee Anne Parker from a baby in a crib. Ashlee Anne's mother was an absent mother in a "Royal" way. Ashlee Anne's mother played tennis, religiously. She watched soap operas, religiously. She took afternoon tea within her social circle, played bridge on Wednesday nights, religiously and was the president and the past president and the past president before that of the Ladies Social Club. Ashlee Anne's father spent most of his time leaning back in his genuine Italian leather CEO's office chair. On Wednesdays he played 18 holes, weather permitting. Miz Lizzie always went on vacation with Ashlee Anne's family. All over Europe, Miz Lizzie did the "help" work and kept the Parkers on pace with their itinerary. Even when Mr. and Mrs. Hemmingway Parker III visited their childhood town, Garrett Grove, Arkansas, Miz Lizzie packed her suitcase before helping Mrs. Parker pack hers.

All along the highway, Oliver played Spanish guitar music for her when they stopped at park benches and rest stop picnic tables. All along the way she would lay across a blanket of grass and listen to Oliver play. He lulled Ashlee Anne deep, then lulled her back out into the great wide open. Each day and each night when the radio frequency couldn't find its way home, Ashlee Anne would turn the radio off and sing in a voice that politely and nicely and honestly confused itself with the voice of Carly Simon. With that voice, she lulled Oliver deep, then lulled him back out into the great wide open.

Oliver and Ashlee Anne, reading to each other as they composed pages of a love story could be heard in their voices. Dancing in Amsterdam fields of red tulips, lost in the sights of a sky full of stars, skipping puddles of Parisian rain, drawing room *Sketches of Spain*, Oliver and Ashlee Anne drove their story on down the road. They were as smooth as Smokey Robinson and the Miracles cruising a Cadillac down the back stretches of Motown. If there was a way to simply put it, it would be simply put exactly like the way it was simply made to be, Oliver and Ashlee.

Their marriage, consummated a day and a half before the wedding, was as good as it gets in a tight space. Two days after they met, they made love, had sex, made love again on the "first date" in the backseat of a crowded 1969 navy-blue black Volkswagen beetle bug. All they had to do was move the guitar case to the shotgun side front seat to block the bright street-light in a Kmart parking lot. Where were they? They were in a small town neither of them could name until they realized they couldn't, when asked, "Do you know where you are?" Neither of them had taken the time to notice what city limit sign welcomed them into town and told them it would be alright to park and have sex in the Kmart parking lot.

Five o'clock in the morning, still pitch-black dark in the Central Time Zone, a nightstick taps on the window. Ashlee Anne had just traded seats with Oliver's guitar case. Oliver had just returned from pissing up against the edge of the dark and was falling asleep behind the wheel. Tap, tap, tap. A policeman wearing a hat too big for his head cited Oliver and Ashlee Anne for Disturbing the Peace in the Parking Lot of a Closed Business. He had Ashlee Anne's VW towed before he took them downtown. Ashlee Anne rode in the front seat next to the deputy, Oliver sat in back behind police car bars. They paid the fine to the deputy in cash because he was also the magistrate after he went into the backroom and put on a black robe. Ashlee and Oliver paid $75.00 to get the towed VW back. Oliver noticed that the last name on the towing company receipt matched the policeman-deputy-magistrate's last name. They still didn't know what town they were in, but by then they didn't care, they were on their way to Palm Springs, California by way of Laredo, Texas.

Out of that town, cruising towards the next town, Ashlee Anne knew well the direction to the next town, Garrett Grove, Arkansas. Ashlee Anne and Oliver were more alive than either of them had been since The Morning of Kmart Magic took a cigarette break, literally fifteen minutes before the citation. They stopped at a truck-stop twenty-five miles outside of the next town. Truck-stop showers are always as hot as you want them to be. Oliver had already showered, changed clothes and was leaning against the VW smoking a cigarette when Ashlee Anne announced her arrival wearing the world around her shoulders like she owned it. Oliver thought twice but did not ask why because she looked so mesmerizingly good. Oliver had no idea that he was already dressed as the only member of the supporting cast, and she was rehearsing her opening lines, dressed for the part leading ladies play. They were getting ready to star in a small-town production.

The complete story of how to rob a bank without a weapon is written in Southern American white woman terminology, but nobody, that day, saw it coming or going except Miss Ashlee Anne Parker. She told Oliver that she would just be a minute, she needed to make a bank withdrawal.

He thought twice without thinking twice as he parked on a side street around the corner from the First National Bank of Garrett Grove, Arkansas. Ashlee Anne Parker got out, brushed her summer white pleats and went for a Mississippi-slow river walk. Strutting Southern-lady-like around the corner, dressed in a white Southern Belle length dress paired with a pair of Mary Janes, white Easter Sunday morning gospel song shoes, Ashlee Anne adjusted her head scarf before putting on a pair of Jacqueline Kennedy Onassis sunglasses. The "Perfect First Lady look" was in place. Then, real slow and Southern-like her reach reached while asking the bank door handle to let First Lady Parker enter.

With an adjustment here and a red lip stick exaggeration there, she knew that she could look as much like any Southern-blonde-somebody-else as anybody going to the bank for lunch that day. She'd rubbed out her fingerprints by smudging lipstick between her thumb and index fingers. The bank camera angle wouldn't be interested in being able to tell Miss Ashlee Anne Parker from any Southern-blonde-anybody-else entering the First National Bank that day at lunch time.

She wasn't the classic "Girl next door." She was beyond that. Miss Ashlee Anne Parker had a Coke bottle figure that figured out how to use itself beyond its full advantage as far back as the first day of middle school. For the world, walking behind Ashlee Anne was a preoccupation or an occupation depending on the time zone in question. Central Standard Time in the middle of the day was perfect. In disarray, according to her sway, the bank security guard knew exactly what time Miss Ashlee Anne Parker walked in and exactly what time Miss Bonnie Parker walked out.

Ashlee Anne Parker stayed married long enough to fall in love with her married name, Parker. So, she didn't give the "Parker" part back to her soon to be ex-husband. She only changed the slant in the way she signed alimony checks and other miscellaneous money matters. She played a stellar-by-starlight role that day. She was up on the drive-in movie big screen. She was watching herself from a seat on the hood of Bad Billy's daddy's Oldsmobile. It was lunchtime at the movies at a three-teller bank in a small Texas town. Two tellers were down the street, eating and gossiping at a lunch break café only a block away.

No one in the history of heists and robberies has ever realized that you can rob a bank without a weapon. If you get caught, what are they going to charge you with, armed robbery? The teller was so concentrated on reading and following to the letter the "This is a robbery, I only want 13 thousand dollars in hundred-dollar bills, no ink, please, I know where you live, I know how many kids you have, I know what school you wish you could afford to send them to," note. Since the lip stick smudged note was written on a bank withdrawal slip, the teller-lady didn't have the space in her head to question how Ashlee Anne obtained her personal information or the time to recognize or analyze that Miss Bonnie Parker, at that moment, didn't have a gun.

The First National Bank Lunch Break Robbery that day went down so smoothly that even the hometown, lunch break customers lined up in line behind Miss Bonnie Parker, waiting to cash checks, to make deposits, to make withdrawals, couldn't tell that they were witnessing a bank robbery. They had no idea that they were watching a movie, *The Crime of the Year in a Small Little Town*. The Garrett Grove businesspeople and homemakers had no idea that Ashlee Anne wasn't who she looked like she was when she walked in and when she walked out. Ashlee Anne walked out with the same Southern genteel, white lady gait that she walked in with, quiet, smooth, swift and in the gaze of the security guard. Her Coke bottle design took his attention away from his duty by design.

When Ashlee Anne sashayed back, the street corner sidewalks recognized her and laid out a red carpet. She turned the corner, mounted the stage, and accepted Oscars for Best Actress in a Crime Drama and Best Criminal Costume Design. The only person Ashlee Anne Parker thanked was Hudson Rivers Oliver. "In less than three days, he gave me the courage to play the part of my life," Ashlee Anne told an audience of street squirrels and lunch time pigeons.

The crime of the day went down in history while Oliver was just sitting there, unaware, without a care, waiting, listening to Johnny Cash on a FM radio station singing *A Boy Named Sue*. He was thinking about the distance between where he was and where he was going. He was thinking about what Tom said in the closing scene of the *Glass Menagerie*, "The longest distance between two places is time."

Then into the light, a little past high noon, walks Ashlee Anne Parker, pretty like the movie star she was. Oliver's face was a two-statement question mark, "That was quick, where to, now, Ashlee?" "Move over unless you want to drive the get-away-car," Ashlee said as normal as a normal lunch on a normal lunchtime, summer day.

Ashlee's answer was a run-on-sentence paragraph, "Without a weapon, I just robbed the First National Bank of Garret Grove, Arkansas . The security guard hit-on me on the way in and harder on the way out. Talk about how a woman uses the shape of her body to hypnotize the eyes of the looker who happen to be a recognizer who does not recognize me. I got $13,000 in one-hundred-dollar bills. As you know, I don't need the money, but I needed to be Miss Bonnie Parker. I needed to tell the audience 'I'm Miss Bonnie Parker, I rob banks.' The teller lady was real nice and she smiled when I told her where we were going for our honeymoon. And when she asked when I got married, I said 'soon.' She couldn't figure out how to smile about that. Everything was easy sounding like a jazz song, Oliver. You taught me how to listen to jazz, you taught me how to appreciate jazz, you taught me how to love the notes in between the notes of jazz."

Frozen briefly in moments of exhilaration, Ashlee Anne softly starts her closing monologue, "And look at you, Oliver, homemade especially for me, dark chocolate, handsome, sitting in middle of a movie made for some late-night looker, trying to pop some more popcorn before the end, not realizing that the movie ends two frames before the end of the show. The authorities will be looking for a Southern belle, a white lady dressed like the First Lady walking out of the White House in the middle of the day, hiking up her dress to get behind the wheel of a navy-blue black Volkswagen bug before driving away. Because they will be looking for the President's wife, a white woman, they will just write it off, if they can't find a white woman who meets the description.

"Believe it when there is no opportunity not to believe, Oliver. Tomorrow afternoon, among a parade of cars of all colors, we will drive past the First National Bank of Garrett Grove, Arkansas and wave to the crowd from the windows of a yellow Volkswagen. We are famous, Oliver, we are celebrities. I see questions in your eyes. Look at you, Oliver, you never noticed the Red River, Arkansas mud I smeared across the license plate, obscuring the numbers, but not the letters just before I took a truck stop shower to wash the mud off my hands."

Ashlee turned left at the light. Seventeen blocks later, she made another left just pass the Colored people section where a Negro sign announced what it announced, but you couldn't hear it if you didn't know how to listen to the Negro side of things. "Bootleg car-paint jobs are always on sale in the Negro section of any city," Ashlee told Oliver as if he didn't already know.

Years ago, when Ashlee Anne's mom and dad moved away from their country relatives and into the city, Ashlee Anne's father got to know Mr. Jesse, an upside-downside Negro with Black businessman's attitude and a disposition that could be deadly if you stepped the wrong way. Nothing was written on any sign because all signs pointed away from Mr. Jesse's place. Mr. Jesse's place was too deep in the hood to need to be written on anything that pointed it out. Mr. Jesse's place sold more auto parts than the auto parts store. Everybody knows Negroes love to fix cars and Ashlee Anne's father made sure they had plenty car to fix. Before he sold all of them and moved to Florence, South Carolina when Ashlee Anne was thirteen, her father owned two new car dealerships and two used car lots in a small town.

You had to know somebody, and somebody had to know you before you could get into Mr. Jesse's Car Paint Factory (fencing) Club. Ashlee Anne Parker's father knew everybody that was somebody in Garrett Grove, Arkansas. Ashlee Anne remembered Mr. Jesse, the only Black man her father referred to as Mister. The connection between the two, Ashlee Anne didn't know, she didn't need to know. Whatever it was, she knew how to use it to her advantage. Mr. Jesse didn't ask about Ashlee's father, he just said, "You still pretty as ever. I can have it ready in 24 hours." Ashlee Anne paid three times the charge in cash, up front and thanked Mr. Jesse with a smile that made cloudy days look for the sun.

Ashlee Anne and Oliver took a yellow cab to the Yellow Hibiscus Motel where there hung a rusted yellow vacancy sign beneath a neon yellow question mark. "If yellow is the color of love, what color did Van Gogh paint the sun?"

Phoebe and Eloise

A dangerously causal smile was his greeting. You could see it in his face from the long distance of being lonely. So, long before they met Jack, they knew him as an uncrowded stage setting, a chair. From day one, the way one sits at a corner table for three was his personality. The song sparrow singing around his neck said he was born in Saskatchewan, Canada, but the angles of his disposition suggested he was from the coast of somewhere as far away as South Carolina. At first, as far as they were concerned, he was nothing more than a Texas roadside silhouette; the kind you see when you drive past Texaco filling stations at dusk and at dawn. His nervous, tenor voice dressed him in rough cut cotton, and there was little breathing room in the way his voice played harmonica during those Dead Goat Saloon evenings that needed music.

From start to finish, they both loved the playful opportunities about him. But all is fair or not fair in love and war. Neither Phoebe nor Eloise took the time to figure out which, so, it's safe to say that Jack's story had no trouble finding its way into the seams and closing scenes of their story, the story of Phoebe Smith and Eloise Wesson.

The Life and Times of a Pistol and a Scatter-shot Shotgun Girl, a true story. But Miss Phoebe and Miss Eloise never admitted that they, truly, saw themselves as such. In royal purple light, they saw themselves as Lady Dame Smith and Lady Wesson, the

Duchess of Whoever . According to one set of rumors, Phoebe wore her diamond on the right hand. According to another set of rumors, Eloise wore her diamond on the wrong hand. Over the years, absence and absent-minded ring fingers decided not to let their hearts grow fonder. So, Phoebe and Eloise took, in stride, their jewelry-store-window life. Phoebe Smith and Eloise Wesson loved window shopping for shiny things.

Too young, but not innocent at all, they both got married the same year in the same church, six months and two days to the day apart. Though neither knew what the inside of a church looked like past seventh grade, they both were religiously in love with roping cattle and cowboys. They both got divorced at the same time of year, a year apart, for the same reason. Harsh phrases, repeatedly, got caught between differences that refused to reconcile. Phoebe cried and cried, took it hard and stumbled out of the matrimony. Eloise was long and tall and nice to look at, so her tears didn't have as far to fall.

It's never been said what Phoebe finally said to the empty space of her empty bedroom mirror the night her world started turning counterclockwise. Now Eloise, regardless of which way her world decided to turn, Eloise would never say such a thing to a rodeo cowboy. Especially if he wore spurs to bed on his alligator cowboy boots, especially if he rode broncos and appaloosas, every night, between sheets made of 100% cotton colored rain, especially if he came in like a Texas size thunderstorm before he went out like a nite-light next to a nightstand.

Phoebe Smith and Eloise Wesson grew up together on the edge of the rural part of the Texas long horn town of Round Rock. There was not a round rock to be found downtown or in the suburbs, so they wondered what kind of round rock town Round Rock was. As young girls, they were intrigued, listening to the weathering purple sounds of raging thunder. Neither cared much for the silence of snow, too slow, so they didn't finish high school at the proper time when all proper girls were supposed to prance across a graduation stage. One absence too many, too many snow days taken without warning according to the weather forecast people and high school principals.

So, about a year after many of their classmates went off to colleges and streets of new city and small towns, it didn't take long before Phoebe and Eloise fell further in love with the size and speed of tornado winds and the hot flatness of flat weather conditions. For the first time in a while, they started skipping the ropes of wearing attention-grabbing short skirts. Somebody noticed how long Eloise's legs were, then out of the blue, that somebody, with his Texas sky sized Layaway Plan, took the time to sell Phoebe and Eloise a General Education Degree Certificate on the merits of not having any credit. They never went to class. They didn't have to because they already knew how to skip school like skipping rope, double Dutch.

They got their GEDs out of the Layaway Plan without paying the first dime. They capitalized on the privilege of being beautiful and almost beautiful. Therefore, they both graduated high school with honors. Their Layaway Plan GEDs landed Phoebe and Eloise at the top of their graduating class, Round Rock High School class of 1979. Because they were supposed to graduate on time like normal, proper girls next door, their graduating class photographs were already alphabetized. S before W exactly where they weren't supposed to be on pages 37 and 43 in the 1979 Round Rock High School Yearbook.

Phoebe and Eloise grew up as groovy girls during a time when the cost of juke box country and western music was nothing but a quarter, a smile and another quarter in the late seventies. And a '77 Ford Thunderbird was the fastest flying bird in town during those days when flight time was short and cheap. They took turns riding "shotgun" in the cockpit of that Ford Thunderbird for as long as they could get away with it. And when they couldn't get away with it, they took turns steering other steering-wheels down dusty back roads of Round Rock.

Phoebe and Eloise, Texas Pete hot sauce hot, teenage girls, flew home with hometown boys on an irregular basis until the night when a Texas heat storm of Harley boys came riding through the ranges of Round Rock. Bad boys, James Dean on a motorcycle, cooler than Steve McQueen in between one of his "bad boy" movies motored in. White t-shirt sleeves rolled up, Marlboros tucked in tight as a pair of tight-fitting blue jeans, faded blue as 1953, straddling the half empty gas tanks of "hogs." According to the thermometer of that summer's Texas size heat, the Harley boys rode out twice as fast as they rode in.

But not before, with anticipation of being Harley Davidson mamas for the time being, Phoebe and Eloise both married the opportunities of listening to hard-boy rock music. Turning Harley Davidson wheels on long stretches of back roads lulled them to sleep, but, by then they had learned to dream in black and white like a movie, like that Barbara Stanwyck picture show, *Double Indemnity* where the leading lady is always the leading lady, but the leading man gets total solar eclipsed into complete darkness.

For some reason, motorcycle tracks never showed up on their small-town road maps. But only in the beginning could that be assumed. Russian cosmonauts with an astronaut attitude, Phoebe and Eloise, in their minds, were the first women to ride on the back of a Harley all the way up to the moon, walk on the face of the moon and make it back to Round Rock with a moon rock not worth being a souvenir. They were spaced in before they got spaced out, at night, gazing at stars, looking for Lucy in the Sky with Diamonds. One hot Texas night they threw their moon rock into the lake to see if it would sizzle. They did not remember Lucy's other name or their young-moon-rock years again, so fondly, until the night they met Jack.

Phoebe and Eloise flew up together like the wingspan-space that separates the wings of a crowd of crows trying to get out of the way of a thunderstorm. Most days, you couldn't slide a sheet of paper between them. They were like clear glue and glass. They were loved by family and there was never any distance in the stars and stares in the eyes of either of their parents. They were beautiful and almost. Phoebe's cunningly cute smile pushed the looker's attention down to how beautiful she was from the points of a tight sweater down to the way she red-painted her toenails. Phoebe's points of reference demanded so much attention, men forget, on purpose, to look into her eyes. Now, Eloise's points were two bra sizes smaller, but her eyes were hypnotizingly bluish green. It was hard to look away from her strawberry blonde, bombshell, Marilyn Monroe way of getting just what she wanted on every occasion she wanted to get whatever she wanted. Eloise wanted everything most of the time. And at times when she didn't want it, Eloise got it anyway.

Miss Phoebe Mae Smith and Miss Eloise Anne Wesson, "Them young ladies were born behind the gun counter of a pawn shop," old ladies used to think, but not say, of them when people thought they were up to no good even when they were up to being as good as they could be.

A middle-class lifestyle behind a white picket fence comes with a manufacturer's suggested retail price. They both learned this in an easy, privileged way. Phoebe and Eloise grew up behind a white picket fence but then drifted away from their white picket fence life in the suburbs of Round Rock. After two marriages, no children and two divorces, they decided to add up everything leftover. Somehow, without looking too closely at the numbers, they decided it was time, again, for them, not so young this time, to be roadway ladies.

Fancy free and in their early forties, Phoebe and Eloise did most of their living during the week. They were always going here and there, so they could spend time apart as the blessing of getting back together. They enjoyed each other's company to the point that it became pointless to complain about spending too much time together. They were like soldier sisters, protecting each other's fortitude and drying up ambition. Phoebe lived on one side of town, Eloise lived on the other, 15 minutes apart during rush hour in a small town. Significant and insignificant others, a relenting question. Over the years, each wrote a long grocery list of potentials, but each potential fell off the bridge because the bridges ice over before roadways during the winter. Phoebe and Eloise were a pair of hard sisters to love. The word must've gotten around before it really had time to get around. So, during the lonesome nights of those early middle age years, Phoebe and Eloise became increasingly intrigued with the idea of blowing up something.

Spherical chrysanthemums, blazing comets, peonies, bottle rockets burst in air, everywhere, a celebration. Life for Phoebe and Eloise could, once again, be like an Independence Night parade with bands marching and spectators watching the majorette tossing a lit-up baton up into the nighttime sky, delighting the joyful screams of children. Yes, they knew life could be spectacular again, but at their age, the fun-of-life was hidden behind something hard to push out of the way like a broken-down car in the road. But that was before they met Jack.

Phoebe took Eloise's advice and Eloise took Phoebe's advice as they had always done and turned fireworks-week upside down and inside out in the wrong and the right direction, simultaneously, one Independence Day night at the Dead Goat Saloon. The Dead Goat Saloon, which had over the years because it was situated just off the interstate, suddenly decided it wanted to be a truck stop. It didn't take long for it to become a favorite place for a few wayward eighteen-wheelers to stop, park and sleep for the night. So, it was one of those firework fortune telling evenings that invited Jack into the dead center of a Dead Goat three-way conversation.

A Dead Goat sight that night lit a pack of firecrackers in Phoebe's mind. The fuses were short, so quickly they exploded when Phoebe told Eloise about how honeybees trick mockingbirds into planting dreams of blueberry bushes in fields where blueberry dreams naturally don't want to grow. "The trick is in the magic of when," Phoebe told Eloise, "Night dreams become daydreams while the blueberries bloom before mockingbirds remember." So, *Dead Fruit on the Bush* became the National Anthem of that evening and many Dead Goat evenings to come. A confused Eloise pretended to understand the illogic of it all, just as she had always done. Listening to Phoebe was like listening to herself trying to make sense out of nonsense. But that was okay because losing Phoebe's insight would be like losing her left eye.

Anyway, that night, several big rig trucks stopped and parked for the night at the Dead Goat Truck Stop. The release of air from the rigs' parking brakes caused Phoebe and Eloise to remember elementary school days when little Tommy Lea used to let them play with his yellow Tonka tow truck every time they would let him play with their Barbie dolls. They were seven years old, and he was six the last time they played with his truck. He was not quite old enough to know the secrets of "Show but don't tell your mommy." So, Phoebe and Eloise only showed little Tommy Lea the inside edges of their secret. As long as he was happy with what he was happy with, they were happy to drive his yellow Tonka tow truck into a head on collision just like good little girls like Phoebe and Eloise were supposed to do when nobody was looking.

That night at the Dead Goat, Phoebe and Eloise weren't looking to find anything substantial buried in the barroom movement of a regular Dead Goat evening. Still, they weren't a bit surprised when they discovered gold. The automobile transport payload of Jack's rig was covered as if it was hiding the identity of a criminal just before a crime was getting ready to happen. The way the payload of Jack's rig was wrapped in plain brown canvas, Phoebe knew there was nothing under that cover but a crime load of pure gold.

In the Dead Goat, Phoebe and Eloise weren't as regular as a lot of the regulars, but they were just as regular as most on Thursday nights. On that retro 1849 California gold rush evening, the Dead Goat Saloon had three eighteen wheelers parked across the street from the Dead Goat parking lot instead of the maximum capacity of two on the dirt side of the road. Crowded parking spaces loved being in full view of Snake, the bartender. Snake's seldom smile was smiling that night.

The Dead Goat neon illumination could be seen from the freeway if you paid attention and knew where to look. Apparently, Jack had a lot of attention to pay, so something in the evening air told him where to look.

The beer was never ice-cold at the Dead Goat, but it was cold enough to always be in short supply and high demand. Still, the beer case's status was all right on any and every Dead Goat night. Anything, most evenings, was all right because a pool table makes just as much ball-breaking noise regardless of the way the 8-ball spins rumors and bar fights. The wayward notions of falling in and out of what some people call love are never loud enough to be heard above the pool table noise. And then, there's the seventeen different ways of misunderstanding the English a pool shark can put on the way a pool ball breaks left or right out into the openness of a one-night-stand table. And then, there's the broken hearts that were already broken before he or she walked into the Dead Goat Saloon, ordered a not-so-cold one, in a hurry, before the world runs out of beer.

A cowboy hat bar and a baseball cap grill, the Dead Goat Saloon did pretty good business without the endorsements of billboards and other commercial entertainment. Everybody already knew everything they needed to know about a Dead Goat's appetite and what was on the menu. Two-top, dark corner tables, four of them, welcomed any and everybody willing put up with ugly tablecloths and ugly plastic center pieces. On the other side of the room, six seating arrangements that don't care how ugly they are, look like they designed themselves from an ugly furniture catalog. And then, there's the three seating arrangements where the married-but-not-to-each-other couples run up silent, secret, discreetly tabulated receipts that show, but please don't tell.

What is the drinking speed of a divorce, how many liquor bottles does it take to make a bar fly, what is the ratio of 1 beer to 2 drops of bourbon, why does it cost more to get drunk in the middle of the day? The Dead Goat's array of Dead Goat characters asks questions, but don't expect answers. They notice everything out of the ordinary without noticing anything inside of the ordinary. Phoebe and Eloise were as ordinary as the regular ordinarys. But that was before they invited Jack to sit with them at their table, placed the long way, beneath a framed straight, hung crooked Dead Goat Vincent Van Gogh *Starry Night*.

Mistletoe shoots more pool than anybody else at the Dead Goat Saloon. Mistletoe shoots pool with a pool stick pointed across the table at wheelchair eye-level. The way he holds his head cocked is a question mark. But make no mistake, that boy has a quick mind. Mistletoe's mama got pregnant after she got pregnant. She was already pregnant when she told a second-story fellow he was the father because the real impregnator had disappeared like magic. The second-story fellow believed Mistletoe's mama until he went downtown to the first floor of the Greyhound station. Mistletoe spends his days rolling around in a wheelchair decorated with a Purple Heart the Army gave him for valor. Mistletoe didn't mean to be brave. A Vietcong sniper cut Mistletoe down out of a Banyan tree. He has been a hung-up-to-kiss-beneath character ever since. Mistletoe was 16, but he told the Army Recruiter he was 18, then showed the Army Recruiter solid proof that the lie he was telling was the God's honest truth. Mistletoe tells lies, loves pretty women and has to have a cheeseburger with his beer, but Mistletoe don't care for nobody's pity.

So, the eyes of the Dead Goat crowd show no pity for Mistletoe. Mistletoe is Mistletoe and you know Mistletoe is Mistletoe when you look into his eyes from the other side of a pool table. Nondependent on which fourth of the dark side of the moon he happens to be on, Mistletoe is always Mistletoe. "Feeling sorry for himself" is too expensive in his game, he never says, but he racks the rack with a fierce force that tells his opponents everything they need to know about Mistletoe. Mistletoe will break you broke, then send you home broke. Yes, if you are stupid enough to want to play 9-ball with a crippled Purple Hearted pool shark, you will have to pay the price of being fooled into believing a straight line isn't always straight. Mistletoe is a straight-shooting pool shark without a conscience. Everything in the Dead is already said about what Mistletoe never verbalizes, "wheelchair-cripped-Purple Heart-tabletop-eye-level angle is a psychological advantage."

Mistletoe's real name is James Miller Johnson. And on some chilly evenings, he parades his Army shirt with his name sown across his heart to prove he is exactly who it says he is. Mistletoe, some people call him Christmas Boy, is an honest farm boy making a dishonest living milking cows bone dry. Mistletoe can make the que ball spin beyond the physics of "rack 'em up, Bud." The sharpest pool shark that's ever been out on the circuit, Minnesota Fats ain't got nothing on Mistletoe Christmas Boy Johnson.

The Dead Goat bartender smokes a pack of Kool cigarettes a day and he is just as cool as he is coldblooded. Everybody knows him as Snake. Snake never says much about anything if it ain't about baseball or football, college and pro. He played second base and tight end in high school. The Houston Astros, Texas A &M, and the Cowboys are Snake's teams. When he's not over-filling and spilling well drinks or washing liquor glasses, he's curled up. Most nights, he's ready to place a sports bet on anything that moves. Like the serpent he is, even at night, from a

Dead Goat's point of view, Snake looks at everything through the lenses of dark sunglasses. Snake looks a little bit like a country boy version of Lou Reed and the Velvet Underground. Snake has never been married. What woman would want to make a livelihood sleeping with a snake in summertime Texas. Some nights, Snake can be as handsome as hurricane season, but, mostly, Snake keeps his variable windspeeds and barometric pressures to himself. That's not to say that Snake hasn't tumbled more than his share of tumble weed women. The fact is, any women who tries to charm Snake, gets charmed right out of whatever she happens to be wearing for the occasion.

Dead Goat locals are typical morning newspaper local folks. Stumble-ins and newcomers are welcome, and Mistletoe does not discriminate against either except on nights when he gets drunk enough to drive his handicap outfitted '77 Dodge Ram van home, drunk. And that's just about 3 or 4 good nights a week, so every policeman and highway patrolman around Mistletoe's side of Round Rock knows Mistletoe's Dodge Ram. The word around town among law enforcement is "If Mistletoe can shoot a straight line, that's fine."

The Dead Goat's eyes never stop hypnotizing the welcoming swing of an opening door. Billy Bob, they call him Curtain Rod, is always at the bar. To the naked eye, it seems Lefty and his boyfriend, Paul, never leave. Lenny and Madalyn, divorced for years, have separate tables on permanent reserve. Shady is always at the bar. Shady's wife is always drunk when she comes in to get drunk and check on Shady. Millie, Curtain Rod's twin sister, only comes in on Wednesdays, Thursdays and Fridays. Miss Ellie Mae Greenway, the schoolteacher, is afraid to sit at the bar, but her estranged sister, a deacon in the church, is a semi-permanent bar stool residence. Hattie Bell and her fourth husband, Andy, keep the bourbon bottles falling like bowling pins most weekends and some weekday nights. Dr. Wasbeen, the history professor, threw darts at any loose woman any night he showed up at the Dead. Phoebe and Eloise sitting at the bar, always on Thursday nights. But that was before that one Thursday night they changed the angle of a Dead center point of view.

The preacher's girlfriend may as well be paying Time-Share rent on the dark corner table tucked behind the pool table, next to the Ladies Room. The preacher never wears a tie when he comes in the back door of the Dead. Snake leaves the back door unlocked on Tuesday and Thursday nights just for him because the preacher doesn't drink in public because he preaches the gospel on Wednesday nights and Sunday mornings. The Dead Goat, nailed to the wall behind the bar, only moves his eyes when he sings along with whatever song is reverberating across and around the contours of the Dead.

The Dead Goat crowd worships the sound garden effects of Hank Williams, Waylon Jennings, Patsy Cline, Brenda Lee and the Coal Miner's Daughter herself, Miss Loretta Lynn. Most evenings, Dolly Parton can carry a whole Dead night by herself. A bushel basket of twang and two-step dance steps tote even and uneven evenings seven evenings a week at the Dead. Johnny and June Carter Cash, a boxing match juke box ring of fire, wild as Ryman Auditorium stage rage. Charlie Pride and Conway Twitty and George Jones and Tammy Wynette turn Round Rock into a square dance. Phoebe and Eloise love juke box quarter music, they love the sound of a quarter dropped in a juke box slot, they love the dull-dim light ambience of a Dead crowd, and they love to shoot 9- ball, but never with Mistletoe. Phoebe and Eloise never shoot 9-ball for money. Small change is too small for them, and big bills are too big to fit in small pocketbooks. But that was before they met Jack.

Phoebe and Eloise's parents got to know each other by mistake. When they were in 9th grade, same homeroom, Phoebe and Eloise made the mistake of skipping school to go early November Christmas shopping. Then they made the fatal mistake of not even going to the mall before they made the fatal mistake of being in the right place at the right time, smoking the wrong brand of nonfiltered, hand-rolled cigarettes. The officer fell in love, momentarily, with Phoebe's pointed profile, but took them downtown anyway. Transfixed, he couldn't figure out how to look into Phoebe's eyes without disappointing his gaze. Eloise's parents bailed them out, got the charges dropped. Phoebe's parents, ultra conservative Christians, cleaned up the house that night and swept the incident and the situation under a cheap Chinese woven rug.

A different stranger shows up at the Dead Goat Saloon almost every weekday night. Weekends are not as welcoming to strangers. The Dead Goat's head never takes the time to notice anything but who's playing what on the juke box unless a fight breaks out. You can look into Snake's eyes and tell he can't wait to straighten out a curve in the road when one does. Snake is a Lake Tahoe desert rattlesnake, not mean at all because he doesn't need to be. Unlike his crooked crawling cousins, Snake doesn't rattle a warning before striking. Willie Lee Bell, a black dude, was the last one to prove Snake's theory of relativity. There hasn't been a black person patron in the Dead Goat since the night Willie Lee thought he was Jesse James or maybe he thought he was Willy the Kid based on what Snake said Willie Lee said before Willie Lee did what he did.

It's unsafe to say, but the regulars that come in through the front door and the back door of the Dead know the real reason Snake bit Willie Lee in his black ass that night. They know it was because of Willie Lee's super pretty, white girlfriend, Kelly Mae Cooper. Kelly Mae Cooper was voted Round Rock High School Home Coming Queen of 1974. She hadn't faded a day according to the way Snake's eyes followed her up and down the bar. In fact, every time Kelly Mae Cooper takes center stage, the dramatics of beautiful moments freeze in place. Snake had a thing for Kelly Mae Cooper. From the first time she and Willie Lee showed up, Dead dark evenings piled up on top of Dead dark evenings. The tension mounted until it became insurmountably crazy in the Dead Goat one night.

Kelly Mae showed back up the same night Jack parked his eighteen-wheeler across the road from the Dead Goat parking lot. Roughly 15 minutes apart, Jack and Kelly Mae entered the Dead. It's a Thursday, the day of the week when the weekend is on the verge of becoming, but not quite brave enough to be weekend redneck rowdy enough to be a full pledged member of the Dead Goat Weekend Club.

And there she was, Kelly Mae Cooper, dressed for the success of the moment, sitting at the bar like being at the Round Rock City Zoo, looking into the eyes of a snake. She was trying to tell venomous from nonvenomous conversation by the way eyes looked back at her. The three point diamond shape of snake's head intrigued her imagination away from thinking about Willie Lee. Willie Lee Bell was no longer in Kelly Mae Cooper's picture. The picture frame had come unglued and fallen from around their love of making late-night love before and after watching late-night classic movies in cheap late-night motel rooms. Their black and white love story started to become unreadable when a Round Rock municipal court judge gave Willie Lee a guilty choice for committing a misdemeanor offense. Willie Lee was accused of and charged with trying to trick the lightning quick speed of vending machine cigarette knobs. The judge told Willie Lee, 'Go to jail or join the Army." Willie Lee decided he would rather be Private 1st Class Willie Lee Bell and jump out of airplanes. Kelly Mae couldn't remember if she told him she would wait for him or not. Willie Lee didn't care one way or the other way because quick as that cigarette knob, Willie Lee found himself a new white girl, not as pretty, but pretty enough for a cougar-lady with money. Kelly Mae Cooper heard all of this through a network of vines, but she didn't tell Snake that part of the story. She told Snake the other part of the story. She did write a long love letter, but she decided not to mail it to Willie Lee because she was still crazy about that crazy black boy.

Six months for a sixty-second ceremony, the thought never entered their minds before it entered their minds with a bang. Phoebe and Eloise came to the Dead Goat every Thursday night like clockwork after a hard day's work. They both worked at the same beauty salon, Dolly's Hair Salon on Maybelle Street. Tuesday through Saturday, they made plain people look pretty with hair dye, combs, curling irons and flat irons. Holidays, weekend engagements and weddings bells love Phoebe and Eloise. They both made pretty good money when you count tips. Still, at this stage in their lives, they both felt used up and laid back like a set of thrift store beach chairs. But that was before they met Jack.

Unpuzzled in life more than they were puzzled by life, still, too many missing puzzle pieces had fallen into the cracks of each of their lives. But somehow, they figured it out like the rapidness of rain, deciding when and where to fall. As two approaching- middle-age drama queens, they figured out how to take the drama out of a dramatic situation, then unnoticed, put the drama back in. Six months for a sixty-second ceremony didn't seem that long at all. A little bird told them that the most dramatic people in the theatre never appear on stage. At first, they didn't believe it.

Getting to know Jack was easy as 7, 8, 9 without consulting the number 10. He told them he drove his rig out of Mobile, Alabama. He told them that he trucked expensive luxury cars from Mobile to Wichita Falls. He told them he was married with two kids, two girls and a boy on the way. His wife was five months pregnant, he smilingly told them. He told them he loved his wife without telling them he loved his wife. Jack's love for his wife was in the slight tremble in his voice when he got lost looking. He told them her name was Anna, and that he stole Anna from the Amish, and then he said, "Just kidding" with a big laugh, big enough to show the liar's gap between his two front teeth. He told them that his father and grandfather were storefront preachers and that his mother was from Farmville, North Carolina. He told them that a neon sign visible from the freeway exit lane told him about the Dead.

How Phoebe and Eloise and Jack ended up sitting at a corner table, eating chicken sandwiches and drinking tall cans of Budweiser was a mystery in motion. Mistletoe figured it out long before it was figure-out-able. But Mistletoe doesn't like to talk, so he never said a thing about the shape of the triangle. All mistletoe knew was that triangles fit nicely in corners. Snake was too curled up in the motion of Kelly Mae to care. The other Dead Goat regulars saw the triangle-talk as just another regular barroom conversation. None but the schoolteacher saw it as it was. Those school children must have worn her out because she was, on her Thursday night basis, sitting at the bar looking in the mirror for reflections of gossip material and school supplies.

The chicken sandwiches at the Dead Goat were Kentucky fried if you took the time to calculate the number of miles between Kentucky bluegrass and Texas dead-brown grass divided by how many times the same grease had been used. But they were good, everybody said so. And everybody knows that truck drivers love home cooked fried chicken and fried pork chops. And Colonel Sanders was in the kitchen at the Dead Goat every Thursday, Friday and Saturday night. Her name is Isabel, but everybody calls her Miss Isabel. Blacker than West Virginia coal, fatter than she wanted to be and sweeter than strawberry wine until you pissed her off. Isabel loves Mistletoe like a son. Don't mess with Mistletoe if you want to stay on the good, sweet side of Miss Isabel Johnson.

Without ever intending to make it a get-me-to-the-church-on-time Sunday morning experience, Thursday nights, every other week became a religion experience at the Dead Goat Saloon. The preacher, sitting in the corner with his girlfriend, praying and saying whatever a preacher says to his girlfriend while sitting at a dim lit table in the corner of the Dead. Phoebe and Eloise and Jack eating chicken sandwiches, drinking tall cans of Budweiser, shooting pool when an open table was open began the way of their night life. Dropping-in juke box quarters, throwing darts at a dart board was target practice many evenings. For almost six months, every other Thursday, Phoebe and Eloise got closer and closer to the eye of the bull.

Some Thursday nights were bull fight nights. Some Thursday nights were flowing red dress nights where lips puckered with the Pamplona red charge of red lipstick made Jack remember the running the Running of the Bulls when he was a young man. Every two weeks on a Thursday night Jack would swing his big rig into a roadside parking space across the road from the Dead Goat parking lot. Jack with his ball cap cocked one way or the other, would walk in like he was walking into his own house after a hard day's work. Phoebe and Eloise would always be there, waiting for the evening tides to come in instead of always going out in unpredictable directions.

Some Thursday nights after chicken sandwiches and tall Budweiser cans, they would rush out of the Dead Goat to catch an 8 o'clock start time drive-in picture show. The three of them loved shoot 'em up cowboy movies with love story endings. Sometimes they would drive Phoebe's long bed Ford around town, other times they would drive Eloise's short bed Chevrolet. Either way, when they went to the drive-in, they would back whichever pickup they happened to roll up in into the drive-in movie space, drape the drive-in-movie speaker over the side, set up three beach chairs, two six-packs of tall Budweiser in cans, a big bowl of home-popped popcorn and enjoy the show beyond what Jack was allowed to know. Certain desires never figured out how to reach their way across narrowness of Jack's tongue, and Phoebe and Eloise only sugar grazed the idea in hypothetical Krispy Kreme cross talk. More than a couple of times they drove right past neon lights of vacancies. More than a couple of times they took Jack out to an all-you-can-eat buffet style restaurant just to see how much Jack could pile on his plate. Jack never realized how quickly he was piling more on his plate than he could eat.

Answers without questions balanced out the three of them. Jack never asked Phoebe or Eloise to promise him anything. He was not bold enough to propose anything like the arithmetic of two plus one. Phoebe and Eloise never discussed the definition of an isosceles triangle. And there were many off-key notes without notice but everything was always understood and silent.

Jack seemed willing to wait, Thursday night after Thursday night, for that drive-in movie night they almost made it all the way to the moon. That night the sky, all the way to the moon, was clear. Her lunar-ness, bold as the axis of symmetry, mirrored a nude full figure that didn't mind looking like a good time to be alive in the bed of a pickup truck. It was haunting in a way. It was one of those nights when the moon dares the looker to look away. Hot, hypnotized moments circling the drive-in movie night atmosphere added to the fire.

Mission control, a hand full of knobs to pull and buttons to push. Launch pad, ready to explode. The countdown speaker voiced 6, 5, 4. Then, as if one of the Goddesses of Weather spoke, it started to rain. Invisible, in the arms of clouds, the moon changed her mind. Mission aborted. Just like that, Jack the Unzipper was back to being Jack up on top of a beanstalk.

All along, Phoebe and Eloise were holding him tight while the sky was falling. From July to December, they danced away the dog days of August, danced through the falling of autumn leaves, danced holiday dances, danced into the first signs of snowfall in Round Rock. They danced to a juke box full of songs. But mostly, Phoebe and Eloise, the cowgirl-two-shooters, two-step waltzed with Johnny Cash, June Carter Cash and Johnny Paycheck. Whatever the dance, the music of the dance was always friendly to the stars in Jack's eyes. Phoebe and Eloise were just as surprised as they were not surprised at all.

When the evening weather decided drive-in movie night was a bad idea, they found other evenings of entertainment. One night they went to the symphony and spent the evening with Ludwig Beethoven's piano concertos. Jack didn't think he would be able to get into classical music, but he did. With Phoebe on his left and Eloise on his right, Jack could get into any place they would take him. Entrance fee for everything, Jack's money was never good enough for Phoebe and Eloise. One Thursday the circus was in town, so they went. They dressed for their parts. Jack was a rodeo clown without the slightest idea of how to get out of the way of a rodeo bull. Phoebe and Eloise dressed as flamenco women. That evening they had the attitudes of three crazy teenagers, crazy in love with the life of the evening. Meandering under the big top world, out for the time of their life, they freelanced. Neither of them good enough to win a prize, but each one of them won a box full of teenage fun and adolescent memories that neither one of them could take back home with them.

Though most evenings were Dead Goat evenings by design, Phoebe and Eloise and Jack counted and courted plenty that were not designed for the purposes of a Dead Goat. Like the evening, they went to Kmart and pretended the three of them were a Mormon couple looking for dresses long enough to cover everything. Or like that late November evening, they venture downtown, Round Rock to partake in the German Christmas Market and got drunk drinking German hot wine. Or like their last, late evening, they all fell asleep in Jack's big rig and woke up the next morning late for work, still dreaming, staring into the dead silent eyes of a Dead Goat sunrise.

And then suddenly like a page ripped out of the story in the middle of being told, the third Thursday in December came, but Phoebe and Eloise did not come in through the doors of the Dead that evening. Jack's disposition, a head full of excuses.

So, it was easy for him to come up with a handful of reasons, way more than he needed. He thought about asking Snake, but Snake had venom in his eyes that evening. He thought about asking Mistletoe, but Mistletoe was in the middle of breaking somebody broke. Besides, Mistletoe don't like people asking him questions. So, Jack picked an excuse from a hand full and tries to live out the evening alone with a tall Budweiser in a can and a chicken sandwich that didn't taste like it was Kentucky fried anymore at all. Isabel must have taken the night off, Jack thought until beneath the barroom lights, he glimpsed her shadow, moving slowly like a ghost, walking across the Dead wood floor.

The first Thursday of the new year came with hints of a snowstorm. Still no Phoebe, still no Eloise. Something must be wrong, Jack thought. Ten every- other-Thursdays in a row, Phoebe and Eloise had been writing stage play parts better than any part Jack had ever been asked to play. Jack looked at the pay phone in the corner of the Dead. The pay phone in the corner of the Dead looked directly back at Jack. That stare-back moment caused Jack to remember that Phoebe and Eloise always promised to give him their phone numbers but made Jack laugh at "How many different ways?" of not giving him their numbers. Jack looked at the telephone book, dangling and frayed. "Hell," he said aloud, "I don't even know their last names." Jack looked at the Dead Goat and the Dead Goat seemed not to be paying attention to moments or minutes at that time. Jack looked at Snake and Snake was smiling the way a poisonous snake smiles at a chipmunk. Then he looked at Mistletoe and Christmas Boy was laughing with a fist full of dollar bills, saluting the evening air like he's holding up Olympic gold. Jack looked at the juke box. The juke box didn't make eye contact with Jack. Something told Jack that the juke box didn't give a damn about Jack if Jack wasn't dropping quarters into her slot.

Texas is a revealing, flattened out, flat-faced state. With all the evidence in his pocket, still, Jack didn't realize that he was the State of Texas' star witness in a crime he didn't know was being committed. Maybe Christoper Columbus was just as wrong as he was right. "The whole world feels just as flat as it feels round," Jack said to himself as he nodded, "See ya later alligator" to a Dead Goat, a Snake and a hand full of Mistletoe branches shot down, again, from a Banyan tree.

The Dead exit door, stubborn as a dead donkey, seemed not to want Jack to leave. Christmas Boy was celebrating, doing a wheelie in a wheelchair, looking for a perfect bank shot to deposit his haul in the Round Rock 1st National Bank. Jack put his head down, pushed hard enough to almost fall, face first, out of the Dead and into the *End Game Surprise*, the closing act. His eyes couldn't believe his eyes. "Where the fuck is my truck?" echoed and echoed. "Where the fuck is my truck?" echoed off into a night of two faces, a mirror and a mirage.

A reflection of him or maybe it wasn't him, John "Jack" Johnson, baptizing the darkness of his own soul music, listening, but not looking, anymore, into the deep dead eyes of a Dead Goat. Jack, the dying star of a tragicomedy dead-danced an unsteady gait. Tears of joy are the same as tears of pain. Rain always falls where it wants to fall. Rain always tells the truth. Jack's face, blank as an unwritten check cashed by a bank teller that didn't care. In the direction of not knowing which way to go, Jack put one foot in front of the other foot. Suddenly, the closing night's carelessness made careful sense. Jack put it all together before it fell apart. So, without further ado, in lieu of Jack, a frightening shadow of dark thoughts voiced Jack's soliloquy.

"I put a spell on you," Jack never knew why Phoebe and Eloise rarely forgot to play the only Black song on the Dead juke box, Nina Simone, most nights of the Dead. "I put a spell on you," Jack never knew what he was listening to.

Jack never knew that Phoebe and Eloise knew that the automobile market value of his haul was close to four quarters of a million dollars. Jack never knew that Phoebe and Eloise knew that the first Thursday in January was the biggest haul of them all, a fleet of one of a kind Cadillac Eldorados and Coupe de Villes bound for Palm Spring's Hollywood egos and out-of-work movies stars hiding out in desert resorts.

Jack never knew that without a single moment of notice, somehow Phoebe and Eloise duplicated the key to his eighteen-wheeler and the key to the key box where keys to the haul are kept. It never crossed his mind that his role was the principal part in an Off-Broadway stage play. The script for the lead role was written on plain as daylight, white schoolgirl notebook paper. It never occurred to Jack to read between the lines.

Jack never knew that Phoebe and Eloise took a big rig, eighteen-wheeler driving course for free for two quarters between July and December. Phoebe bribed the instructor with the accumulated point value of the points beneath a thin, sky colored, summer blouse. They showed the community college admission officer some prettied-up copies of some official looking papers. In less than five months, Phoebe and Eloise learned to drive an eighteen-wheeler in the dark.

Jack never knew that Phoebe Smith and Eloise Wesson knew he had no pregnant wife back home named Anna Renee. They knew that his Anna Renee was not an escapee from whatever Amish village Jack laughed about. They knew on his days off, he no longer picked up his kids from public school. They knew that by fatal mistake and child support payments that he lived alone in a one-bedroom apartment and that he used to have the keys to a three-bedroom, three-bathroom suburban address on his key ring.

Jack never knew that Phoebe and Eloise knew that honoring the kindness of a shark is the finest of all fine arts. He never knew that their playbook was the handbook of a grifter, and it was a smooth read, smooth as the opening scene becoming the closing scene of a 3-way heist.

Jack never knew that Eloise and Phoebe knew that he would

never lead the crime scene to the doors of the Dead. They knew he would never allow the yellow tape crime scene tape measurers to park their crime scene vehicles in the parking lot of the Dead. Jack never knew that Phoebe and Eloise knew he would never tell the investigating committee of officers "Who dun it."

From the opening curtain to curtain call, the most dramatic people in the theatre, Phoebe and Eloise, never appeared on stage. Jack took a bow. The theater audience's applause, a standing ovation, loud enough for Jack to hear above and below the echoes of "Where the fuck is my truck?".

Walking in any direction that leads away from the Dead. Dead reckoning in the dead zone of not knowing, Jack looked up and measured the size and shape of the full moon. In the middle of the longest moment in his life, Jack counted the number of seconds in an hour by multiplying the number of minutes in the moment that waited to reveal that no more than 17 miles away, the same full moon looked down upon two roadway ladies blowing down the road like Texas tornado wild wind women as the fastest truck-route to Mexico City, Mexico kept getting faster and faster.

Dark clouds twisted the shape of the night. Un-constellated stars folded their brightness into a circle the size of a baby sun. Ursa Minor, the Big Dipper's handle, broken off and falling up into a higher darkness. Outside of the Dead, Venus cried on the shoulders of Mars.

Tilted to a deeper shade of sadness, the sky seemed sorry. As sad as the end of Jack's story decided, without notice, to end, Jack was smiling while sliding off the edge of the earth. Walking in darkness by moonlight, Jack's smile was careful not to trip and fall. Jack's smile was looking up at the truck-route to Mexico City moon, the same full moon. But it wasn't the same full moon. Jack was at a drive-in picture show, looking up into the night sky before the rain came, the night the three of them almost put a triangle around the moon.

Pawn Shop Blues on Guitar

Of course, Mrs. C didn't mean to pawn her husband, and of course she didn't mean to walk through that door that day the way one walks, politely, into a pawn shop carrying an acoustic-electric guitar like it was an upright bass. Blame it on her car. Her Volvo convertible decided she was hungry, so it parallel parked in front of a Pentecostal storefront church across from the Sad Ballard Café Buffet next door to Guns and Pawn. "We Take Just About Anything," the pawn shop logo announced, but Mrs. C couldn't be sure she heard what she heard. The sky was an angry royal blue that early afternoon, so after a scary salad lunch, she ventured next door through the exit door to see if what she thought she heard was what she actually heard. A seeing-eye dog wearing a MINGO name tag was the only one to smile upon her arrival as if that Standard Poodle knew how standard that day would turn out not to be.

Of course, she didn't mean to pawn her husband at the same pawn shop sixteen or seventeen times, she can't remember, over the course of their3 ½ year marriage. But maybe Mrs. C did mean every moment of this and every minute of that seeing as to where she comes from and how she was raised on the richer side of a rich mountain. Communities of rich strangers that know each other, only, by the number of dollar bill signs in the air is where she's from. "Our Town," as Mrs. C calls it, where it rains when it's supposed to rain, and it snows at Christmas time by request.

Of course, the streets of her "Our town" were not literally paved in gold, but literally they could be paved in copper. If one were to take the time to blow the dust off all that "old" money banked in memories of the "the Old South," take all those hundred-dollar bills down to a Walmart coin counting machine, hit reverse and let it spit out shiny copper pennies, day and night, for about 2 years, one could copper-pave the Story of Scarlett O'Hara, pre- 1859. Antebellum, the way magnolia trees and live oaks shaded walkways, Mrs. C remembers her childhood with fond patience. Growing up, pawn shops and flea markets and yard sales were so far beneath her, so deep in the valley, she barely knew any of them existed. Now, without any notice that she has noticed, she walks headlong, engulfed in circles of scared determination, into a pawn shop breeze. She has fallen in love with the rhythms of pawn shop blues.

Of course, Georgia summer mountain weather is always a little cool, especially at night and of course down-in-the-valley pawn shop sharks always swim in formation and smile when they see her-side-of-the-mountain people (though she's the only one) enter through that *Y'all come back now, ya hear* pawn shop door. Pawn shops are always located in places that raise questions and always on the other side of any town. And they are almost always crowded with customers who look the parts they play, forever trying to construct or deconstruct the inflated value of a ten-dollar bill. So, it's no wonder every customer looks up when Mrs. C enters, carrying her suit jacket husband the way one carries something freshly pressed when one leaves the dry cleaners.

Of course, the voice of "Love Me Tender" and "Are You Lonely Tonight" leaves her crying in the aisle. And of course, all of Mrs. C's songs slow dance that "slow Southern style." On her veranda, while heat and humidity race toward three digits, mint juleps and sweet tea pour themselves over ice. Every afternoon, a new religion permeates the lack of breeze jumping softly between shadow and shade. Mrs. C feels the music blow through her platinum blonde hair. A Volvo convertible, sour apple green, a straight stretch of road, she is the epitome of a Southern belle. Hair pulled back, wearing big sunglasses that look in the mirror at themselves before looking in the mirror at her. She's exactly who she's always been. Like a debutante from a bygone era, she still has her dance card. And she's still looking for that semblance of a J. Gatsby ballroom on a sweaty, August night. She can still see rows of ceiling fans fanning, turning time like time is standing still. She can still feel the palm of a handsome hand asking her, "May I have this dance?" She can still smell the ambience, the Southern charm of being chased. She has always been an open-window daydreamer. From time to time, even downtown in the middle of the day, Mrs. C always looks up because she loves the opulence of big chandeliers hanging from ballroom ceilings. She wondered if pawn shops sell ballroom chandeliers in the back rooms of ordinary life. Whatever that is, she thinks.

Of course, she didn't mean for her husband to be pawn-shop-poster boy. Of course, she never took into consideration that he played a right-handed guitar upside down and backwards because he was left-handed and he left this and that in the wrong place, most of the times, for the same reasons she never took the time to understand. She didn't need to. She grew up rich enough not to have to understand anything.

Of course, in high school, they liked the same kind of music, so they got married one senior summer night in the back seat of a blue Range Rover. Ironically, 9 ½ years after that fact, they remarried in a church with two steeples, one visible to the naked eye, the other not quite so. From the start her family accepted him on paper without accepting him in print. But she breathed every moment of him and loved him until the perfume became too strong for her to smell. From the start, her father said "Why," and her mother said "Try." Now at 33, the question begs itself: "Rich Bitch or Wealthy Lady?" She knows, only, that she's a cliche either way her Southern breeze decides or decides-not to blow.

Of course, they wanted kids and of course around Christmas time they wanted kids even more, but that's another story that has nothing to do with the square footage of a pawn shop or how she loved playing with toys. Nathan, he was a pretty boy. She thought he would make pretty babies, but pretty-soon was too soon, wrong . Adoption Agencies, always question marks. They didn't want to adopt for reasons neither one of them was willing to talk about after she quit listening, the moment he picked up his guitar. So, it's safe to say that that day when she took him to the pawn shop earlier than usual, it had been a long time since she had heard him sing his song.

Of course, if you've watched pawn shop reality TV, you know pawn-shop-people are funny people. With a smile that's not really a smile, they always ask, "How much ya want for it?" And the customer always says, "Are you willing to go as high as...?" The crazy one-up, one-down exchange rate of pawn shop blues, but it wasn't anything like that for her. She didn't need the money, just the music, and the pawn-shop-people knew because she always walked in like she was walking onto a yacht even when she was wearing yoga pants with her Tai Chi top, carrying her suit jacket husband like carrying weight without gravity.

Of course, everyone assumed Nathan had just been pawn-shopped again when he didn't show up for work that week. But, more than any of them knew, this time when Mrs. C wanted to get rid of her husband for a while, Mrs. C figured out how to get rid of him for good. In all fairness to the pawn-shop-people, she was headed towards the pawn shop that day. Somewhere along the way, her mind changed her, and she ended up at an out-of-town car dealership. She didn't know she could do it, but she did. She walked right in wearing a different pair of yoga pants, but the same Tai Chi top, signed all the papers and traded her suit jacket husband in for the only used Tesla they had on the new car lot. She told the new car salesman to tell the used car saleslady to tell her suit jacket husband that he could have the Volvo convertible as partial compensation for a dishonest mistake. She'd read somewhere that "All is fair in love..." She didn't remember the "and war" part on purpose. "The keys are on the console, and I left it running," she yelled against the super quiet start of her new used Model S, Midnight Cherry Red Tesla.

Of course, she was happy and, of course, she was sad. "The Way She and Nathan Never Were" was playing on the radio, a Willie Nelson song. The sky wasn't angry that afternoon, wasn't royal, anymore, either. And as if "just looking" could finish telling a story, a day-time crescent moon could be seen, only, if you looked straight into her hazel tinted eye shadowed eyes as she touched up her makeup in the rearview mirror. She was thinking about highchairs and tricycles and training wheels and trampolines and cartwheels and somersaults and the sound of children laughing. And of course, then, drifting, she drifted back to the price of Renaissance oil paintings and caviar and champagne and ballroom chandeliers and the sad, flat straightness of her platinum blonde hair. Sitting at a stop light intersection, a question softly, sadly, lingering-ly touched, lightly, her bare shoulder. Left on green or right on red? Of course, she did not know which way to turn.

Station Wagon People

Not sure if it was coincidence or not, but it was, without question, ironic that both their fathers drove 1958 blue and white Ford Del Rio, full size, six passenger station wagons with plaid pleated fender shirts. It was also ironic that the station wagons parked themselves in driveways of split-level, white picket fence houses directly across the street from each other. Thus, it was not ironic at all that the taillights of one Ford Del Rio faced the taillights of the other Ford Del Rio on a nightly basis. Weekend parking space was anybody's guess for reasons the station wagon people felt no need to explain.

"It was a beautiful time to be alive," the technicolor color television set said every night three or four times during commercial breaks. Children were not allowed to change the television channel if an adult was in the room. Parents still remembered listening to the radio after supper with their parents. All the parents walked for miles to get to school if you listen to them tell the story. The parents were Great Depression-era children and they remembered what their parents called Hoover times. They didn't care much for his wife, but they loved FDR. Some day for them, Franklin Delano Roosevelt was God.

White bread, meat and potatoes were always on the supper table just in time, waiting for fathers and grown sons to take off their working boots. The people loved the factory just a little bit more than they hated it. Christmas bonuses put the delight of receiving smack dab in the middle of the margin of error. Most of the boy kids collected baseball cards and shot marbles for keeps. Most of the girl kids played with Barbie Dolls until they were old enough to wear Bobbi socks with their saddle shoes and above-the-knee pleated skirts.

Every summer, both their fathers packed kids, wives and suitcases in station wagons and drove endless miles to nice, affordable vacation places. There they stayed four or five days, then packed up kids, wife and suitcases in station wagons and sightsaw their way all the way back home. Both their fathers worked at the same edge-of-town plastic pollution-making plant, ate the same thing for lunch at least three times a workweek from the same kind of beat-up lunch bucket pail, and drank the same kind of beer every night of the week, Budweiser, tall cans, the King of Beer.

Tommy and Tommy lived across the street from each as far back as either could remember and beyond. They both had two younger sisters, Heidi and Elke and Marie and Johanna. Tommy and Tommy turned 14 years old in the first part of December 1963. President John Fitzgerald Kennedy was still fresh on everybody's mind. "Texas is an unkind state, and Dallas is an ugly-minded city," it seemed the whole town thought without saying. The mood in their part of Phoenixville, Pennsylvania that time of that year was blanketed in sadness and snow.

It was kind of easy to tell that even the people who didn't like the Bostonian voice of Jack Kennedy loved the sound the letters J-F-K made when they said his name out loud in the corners of their private backrooms. On Tommy and Tommy's side of the world, it seemed the people didn't care what anybody had to say, the pronunciation of the L-B and J didn't sound enchantingly, intriguingly beautiful like the pages of Camelot they'd come to love whether they read the chapters or not. Tommy K. saw his mother cry for the first time the day Lyndon Baines Johnson of the ugly state of Texas took the Presidential Oath away from

Jackie and Caroline and little John John. At least it was the first time he'd felt the weight of his mother's tears as they rolled down her cheeks onto the kitchen table like small puddles after rain.

They were nothing alike, at least, that's what everybody said. Though they both were suburban housewives, they both loved their Hoover vacuum cleaners, they both delighted over the colors of their modern appliances: summer mint green refrigerator, canary yellow stove, Tommy and Tommy's mothers were nothing alike. Tommy Z.'s mother was Jewish with laughing, loud-talking, reddish hair. Her black cat-eye eyeglasses angled her secret Gelsenkirchen smile. Angled her smile to the point that her smile was almost hidden if you didn't look close enough to see her twisted smile lines. Tommy K.'s mother had shortish, quiet, straight, dark hair and was said to be Black Irish. Of course, that wasn't common knowledge because she wasn't supposed to want it to be common knowledge since there wasn't a hint of darkness about her complexion. In fact, she was whiter than she was supposed to be. Tommy K.'s mother wore her life like a library book wears a dust jacket, waiting to be checked out, returned late with an overdue notice stamped, UNPAID. Secrets in a garden town grow like tomatoes on tomato vines. But the world knew that Mrs. Wolfgang and Mrs. Dietrick knew more about each other than their soap opera afternoons would ever admit. *As the World Turns* came on every day of the housework week at 1:30 EST on CBS.

Mrs. Wolfgang and Mrs. Dietrick's respective sons, Tommy and Tommy, were born in the same Phoenixville General Hospital 46 minutes apart. One before midnight, the other after midnight. One Tommy's cord was cut a quarter 'til the clock stuck twelve, the other Tommy's cord was cut two quarters and a minute after the clock stuck twelve. No question, Tommy and Tommy were twins, people who didn't know them thought for sure.

At 14 years old, Tommy and Tommy were about the same height, same weight, same build. They both wore the same size 9½ shoe, but if you looked at their feet long enough, you could tell their shoe size had a lot more growing to do. Both boys had dirty blond, wavy, unusually unruly hair. They both had unpiecing hazel-brownish eyes. They were both on their junior high baseball team. They both wore left-handed baseball gloves. They both batted on the right side of home plate. They both rarely figured out how to steal second base. They both were pretty good infielders, one at second, the other at short stop or third. The last game of the season that year, they both grounded out twice and struck out twice before Tommy Z. hit one out of the park saving a losing season.

They both were C minus students in every subject except subjects that didn't have anything to do with anything that mattered like sneaking into the movie house, smoking cigarettes, and shuffling playing cards. They both liked cowboy television shows and any kind of war movie. They could both climb trees like Tarzan, outrun jack rabbits and shoot BB guns like trained soldiers. They both had never been on an airplane. They both had fathers that were first generation German American. They were both in love with the same girl next door. They both had never seen the ocean in person.

Together, side by side, they looked alike, but not so much that one couldn't tell them apart. But in the eyes of a stranger who saw one of them at the drug store and later saw the other one walking past the barber shop, they were identical twins, you couldn't tell them apart. When talking about Tommy or Tommy, people who knew them distinguished them by the first letter in each Tommy's middle name. Thomas Karl Dietrick was Tommy K, and Thomas Ziegler Wolfgang was Tommy Z . Tommy K. and Tommy Z. dressed alike in that they dressed, mostly, in classic '50s fashion when they could afford to and, ironically, when they couldn't afford to. Like the older boys, they wore three-quarter length car coats, white socks, rolled up Levi's, white tee shirts and penny loafers with pennies in the slots. Their ogling eyes belonged to girls who wore saddle shoes and bobby socks with their timeless skirts, loose in typical mid-century style. In their heads, but not necessarily on anybody else's mind, Tommy K. and Tommy Z. were as cool as James Dean and Steve McQueen that last part of fall, 1963.

Her name was Oleander Anne Smith. She was named after a flowering bush and the flowering bush she was named after didn't grow native in their hometown. So, according to the gossipy air that blew about and beyond the neighborhood, she was an immigrant, so to speak if one were to speak of such matters. No one ever said a thing about it loud enough to be heard and besides she didn't mind being foreign, as far as Tommy Z. and Tommy K. could tell. Most of their attention was paid to the way Miss Oleander Anne Smith walked up a flight of stairs. "Stairway to Heaven" was a Neil Sedaka, rock 'n roll song in 1963.

Tommy K. was out-of-his-mind in love with her Swedish blonde hair. He paid Clark-Kent- close attention to the silent, graceful way Oleander Anne's hair touched her shoulders without touching her shoulders. It was like glistening strands of sunlight brush-kissing one shoulder, then the other shoulder when she turned her head this way, then that way. They knew Oleander's hair was Swedish blonde because the girl that did the Swedish soap commercials on Tommy K.'s new color television set had hair that was the same color as Oleander's hair. From the other angle, Tommy Z. really loved the color of Oleander's eyes. The air that floated around the contours of her Scandinavian shaped face woke him up in the middle of the night some nights. Contrary to nothing anybody would try to understand, they both loved, absolutely, everything about Miss Oleander Anne Smith except that she never paid either one of them the slightest bit of extra attention regardless of how hard they tried to lock eyes with her for the sake of being able to say so.

But that's the way it's probably supposed to be, they thought uniformly, when they were not thinking about how movie-star beautiful Oleander Anne Smith was when they saw her anywhere, but especially when she came into the Welcome to Winn Dixie grocery store where Tommy K. and Tommy Z. worked as bag boys on the weekend and as stock boys during the week. Sometimes during the week when Tommy K. was stocking shelves, measuring the sacred space between rows of merchandise and she walked past, he noticed how cans of green peas begged to trade places with packages of dry lima beans and spaghetti noodles. "It's all about vantage point and who or what is doing the looking," he was always too entranced in his other thoughts to think. On the weekend when Tommy Z. was bagging groceries and she was standing in the checkout line, he couldn't get chicken breasts and hamburger meat to fit into the same doubled paper sack without the sack splitting down one side or the other. "It's all about shape and volume," he was too preoccupied to remember.

Then, when one spring came, Oleander decided to bloom early just to get it out of the way of her May Day graduation from high school. Then, when the twins heard she had applied for college in another town, they couldn't imagine working in a grocery store where Oleander didn't come in twice, sometimes three times a week to buy beer and cigarettes and other grocery items for her family. Somebody told the twins years ago that Oleander's mother lived in a wheelchair and spent most of her days on the front porch talking to anyone and everyone that walked by their address, #17 Casper St., NW. The twins knew Oleander's mother's sister lived with them. The twins knew, also, that Oleander didn't have any brothers or sisters, but they didn't know why she didn't have a father.

Roosevelt Junior High located itself next to Roosevelt High on Shadow Street, so some days when the last bell of the day rang, the twins would try to make it over to the where the high school students were milling around after school. They were looking for a chance to walk a few paces behind Oleander as she walked home. This adventure mostly proved fruitless because like jewelry, a small, silver crowd lived around Oleander's neck, always. She seemed to always be in the middle of two or three talking while walking conversations.

Heidi and Elke and Marie and Johanna weren't allowed to cross the street to play with each other until they were old enough to look both ways. Three of them were in the same second grade class. Elke was an advanced child, so she was elevated to Advance Class. Tommy Z. remembers how scared his parents were that he would not make it out of fifth grade. Tommy K. does not remember his parents being overly concerned that by the grace of God and Jesus, he made it out of fifth grade. Tommy and Tommy were space cadets, and they both cruised day in, day out ever since President Kennedy said he was going to put a man on the moon by the time Tommy and Tommy graduated from high school.

Ordinary days in their ordinary, blue-collar town were ordinary most days. But that late Tuesday afternoon wasn't ordinary at all. Tommy and Tommy were taking a break behind Winn Dixie. They both sat on the tall end of Coke crates. They were smoking cigarettes, Pall Mall Reds with no filter to filter out what didn't need to be filtered out. Sitting there, they had no idea a storm without wind or rain was impending. And if they had ever been told the truth, it would've taken the whole town to convince them that it wasn't a lie. But it was true. Their 10-minute break was 9 minutes and counting towards lift off. The cigarette butts were starting to burn the tips of Tommy and Tommy's fingers.

It was one of those gossip-line exchanges that everybody exchanged except everybody. Neighbors that knew didn't know. Even the milk man and the mail man knew but didn't care to know the details. Yet, it was anybody's knowledge that Tommy K.'s and Tommy Z.'s fathers were typical, like so many of the other factory-working fathers, weekend alcoholics and summertime cookout artists. Everybody knows everything, small towns always think. But they didn't know what only Tommy Z.'s mother knew. Tommy Z.'s father loved time-and-a-half overtime pay more than he could ever bring himself to love her, his wife of twenty-some years. To hear Tommy Z.'s father tell it, he fell asleep sober and woke up the next morning, drunk, on the other side of the world. Not so deep in the convincing color of Oleander's eyes, you can tell Tommy Z.'s father still loves a woman he loved overnight 18 years ago, a woman, now, in a wheelchair who still lives on a street where ghosts are still friendly to people they know, and when the weather's good, clothes still hang on clotheslines in the backyards of summertime from time to time.

Tommy K. had just finished stocking shelves and was bagging groceries. It was 10 o'clock am. It was the third weekend in June. Apparently, Miss Oleander Anne Smith decided not to shop for cigarettes and beer and other grocery items that Saturday morning. Somehow, the earth seemed too quiet in the wrong place, seeing that the Winn Dixie parking lot looked like an impending holiday. Of course, every car in the parking lot wasn't a station wagon, but every car in the parking lot, from a distance, appeared to be a station wagon, packed up, ready to get out of town.

Time-clock time didn't care how many hours got worked and by whom, it seemed. Tommy Z. hadn't shown up for work. Tommy K. didn't even bother to guess why because it wasn't even ironic anymore that chicken breasts and hamburger meat didn't even pretend-try to get along. They didn't care. Brown paper sacks didn't care. They simply decided to split along all seams simultaneously as if they knew the end of the world didn't care. Tommy K. didn't care anymore either, how could he? He wasn't thinking to himself, he was thinking out loud, "If she's Tommy Z.'s half-sister and I'm Tommy Z's twin, what then?" The cashier girl, Missy, answered Tommy K.'s question with a question. "Didn't Mr. Rodgers tell you to always put chicken breasts in one doubled brown paper sack and hamburger meat in a separate doubled brown paper sack," Missy almost yelled over the complaining voice of a valuable customer as the doors of the Welcome to Winn Dixie flew wide open and Tommy Z. blew in like a late wind.

Dancing at the Hot Flash Club

As I danced the sky-blue afternoon away and right into the middle of the tight fit of my sadness, the question was what did the six of them think of the one of me driving a 16-year Mercedes convertible with my hair slicked back like the Mafia.

Well, the definition of what used to be me, and perhaps still is, goes back almost two years' worth of full moons ago. Were they able to see that far back? If so, what did they really think of me in the haze of blue afternoon mimosas and screw drivers.

Signs of a wasted life must have been written not on my face, but in the way the six of them watched me moved against what turned out to be a welcoming Virginia blue afternoon wind.

But back then, a few of those hard-marriage-years ago, the same wind with a different name and a different attitude watched out for me. Now, that same west blowing wind still blows every time I turn my head to look back over my left shoulder at the way things were when love pretended to like me. As if that's not enough, it really blows every time, I drive my Mercedes down suburban neighborhood streets of nice houses with manicured lawns and I spot that one nice house that looks like it needs me and my dear John Deere to stop by and cut the grass.

Our twenty-seven and half month married life was pretty good until it wasn't. We were happy until we weren't. Norma Jean started out being a good love maker, a good home maker, but a bad cake baker. She never made a birthday cake for me.

She hired a cleaning lady to do the housework and I took care the curb appeal.

Some Saturday or Sunday mornings were often summertime, lower middle class classic scenes. Like the times when I wore classic Clorox beach white "wife beaters" routinely on those routine weekend mornings. Front and center, there I was, a white "wife beater" gall shirts wearing stereotype, a question mark man. But maybe that kind of cotton shirt arithmetic gives the wrong answer on purpose, especially on Sunday mornings when cutting the grass or going to church is simultaneously the right and the wrong way to go if you are headed in the direction of being saved at a Sunday morning soul saving station.

Yet, categorically, at any point in the story of Norma Jean, I can say, definitively, that she used to read me like a terribly interesting, badly written novel. Every third page was dog-eared one way or the other way. She never would underline what the dog-ears were pointing towards or away from. The only thing I am certain about, which is still uncertain most days, is that the direction, size, speed and shape of our relationship determined which mathematical model of Mercedes I drove away driving when driving into a world of no trade-in value car dealerships.

Anything that looked like love back then must've been love. And so, if a lot of what I say sounds mixed-up, it is mixed-up. I am trying to sort some things out this afternoon. So back to the future or back to the past, I have never been able to tell left hand love from right hand love. They are the same, to me, depending on if you know where the equator is supposed to be according to the geography of a trailer park double-wide world.

I grew up as a peculiar kind of redneck, white boy. I was born in a trailer park village that didn't know it was trailer park trash, as they say. Our red dirt trailer park village thought it was a 17-acre, double wide condominium luxury parking lot. So, with that upper class way of seeing herself, our trailer park land lady told us that our necks were not red enough to be classified as authentic rednecks. She said, although we were still low-class citizens, it was quite permissible for us to listen to classical music when no one was looking.

I grew up religious in a trailer park kind of way. That is to say, people who didn't go to church on any given Sunday, didn't show their faces until church services were over. That probably accounts for why I cut the grass wearing a "wife beater" many married life Sunday mornings. Our trailer park landlady, also, told us that we could call Mozart or any of the three trailer park, doublewide Jesuses depending on who was on call when we needed to call somebody to help get us out from in-between some kind of indecision.

It is a solidly stated fact that for twenty-seven and a half months, I was married to a woman from the other side of my trailer park railroad tracks. Norma Jean had upper-middle-class class. Any class I had was adopted class. We lived in a white with green trim, 1950s style ranch house with a sizable yard. It was as natural as it was normal some summer-time Sunday mornings to cut the grass when the grass was tall. Yeah, I would be out there sweating through two white "wife beaters," trying to sweat out a couple of 6 packs of Saturday night Bud Light.

But, Norma Jean Smith, she never changed her name, was the real relationship "beater" in the family. Every morning, she beat me to the shower, to the coffee pot and out the door. Every lunchtime in the relationship declining months, she had a different lunch date and every evening, she beat me in the racetrack ride not to do suppertime dishes. And, get this, she used to beat me up with a whip, decisively, every time I tried to chess-checkmate her into telling mesome current version of the truth of who her other significant others were or were supposed to be. To the best of my knowledge, my best guess is three.

And, yes, I know she's still a chess playing playboy bunny full of negligee night life tricks and unpredictable daylight stratagems designed to confuse who ever she's happens to be with into believing that if she wanted to, she could climb up into the saddles and ride both white *knights* and both black *knights* to the moons around Jupiter and back with one chess move. She had me wrapped around her black and her white *bishops*. Her *queen* always had total control over each *rook*, and it took an act of science and an act of God and an act of congress to checkmate the *king* of Norma Jean.

We grew up playing checkers and chess when we weren't playing baseball and football in the field behind our trailer park neighborhood. I thought I was a pretty good chess player until I got married. It was then that I learned that the power of a black *king*, a black *queen*, two black *rooks*, two black *bishops,* two black *knights,* two black *bishops* and eight black *pawns* was not enough power to react to Norma Jean's opening move. Norma Jean always figured out, in advance, how to get the white pieces. In chess, white always has the first move.

But I got out of that unholy matrimony with a lot less than I came in with, so I won't confuse you or defuse you with the minute details of her until-death-do-we-part personality. But I will tell you this, which accounts for about ¼ of one reason I stayed for as long as I did. She was crazier than the story I am about to tell you. Listen, she told me that her great grandmother told her that a man only needs two pairs of socks, a pair to put on and a pair to take off.

I walked out of that marriage with the gait of better days, wearing both pairs of my original socks because it was too cold for one pair with holes in the big toes. And besides by the time I left, I had three pairs of Alphonso Capone, Pretty Boy Floyd, genuine leather Italian shoes. I was compelled by a certain fashion statement to invest in a few pairs of cotton silk socks. What kind of shoes and socks do you expect a trailer park boy with a classical music IQ to wear when he motors away, driving a sixteen-year-old Mercedes up and down friendly streets. Of course, Norma Jean never had any idea about the nature of what was in my sock drawer and of course I didn't tell her everything I am telling you and of course I probably won't ever tell her about the hormonally hampered heroines I danced the afternoon away with at The Hot Flash Club.

Somehow, momentarily, I must have forgotten the real reason I was still, as I see it, dancing in the twilight zone of that Thomas Jefferson, Virginia afternoon. Marriage is a funny thing if you look at it upside down and sideways. Marriage always works in retrospect. And you probably realize that if you look at marriage in retrospect for the rest of your life, it will last the rest of your life. And you will be the senior partner in a good ole, happily married couple on the couch wearing re-runs and watching re-runs, laughing at the routineness of big screen TV dinner evenings. But the very moment I looked at my marriage right side up, it was gone like a cool Chuck Berry breeze, circa 1962. In fact, Chuck Berry and Jerry Lee Lewis were singing a free concert on somebody's transistor radio that blue afternoon of the walking kitchen tour.

Two fortnights, one weekend and three days to the day I left the town that married me, then broke me, I broke the speed limit faster than my sixteen-year-old Mercedes wanted to go into the outer spaces of another town. I was a NASA trained astronaut on Saturday, July 27, noon to 4pm. I was dressed up like a both-sides-of-the-moon excursion.

That blue afternoon, The Virginia Highlands Festival invited me on a tour. It was an annual tour, A Walking Tour of Distinctive Kitchens in the Sweet Bay area. The announcement was posted straight as Norma Jean's night black lace in a sideways hotel room on a sideboard building located where Second Avenue crosses Main Street. The announcement announced like a loudspeaker, "$40.00 per person." A kitchen tour, what the…? I was thinking about how Norma Jean decorated our renovated kitchen with the way she wanted to makeup her face to look when she stepped out into the nightlife streets of our town. Lipstick tubes of lip gloss, fake eyelashes, mascara, blush brushes, all positioned, competing with forks and spoons and knives for countertop drawer space. Powder room makeup bottles and face cleansing pads paid the cleaning ladies no attention whatsoever.

So, in the middle of a sky blue afternoon, cruising the outskirts of a new town, a kitchen decoration show was the last place I wanted to go, but my sixteen-year-old Mercedes convertible and four Abraham Lincolns and one Andrew Jackson in my front pocket of my cotton tread pants decided that I didn't know what I was about to miss out on.

So, I stepped right up and paid the cost to be the boss like B.B. King talking to his guitar-woman, Lucille. Sometimes being in the wrong place at the right time is a sweet blessing that doesn't know how to disguise itself as anything else but what it is on a sky-blue afternoon.

Something out of the blue put a little music in the way, so I couldn't get by without listening to the sounds of high heels strutting across linoleum and hardwood kitchen floors. Trying not to remember the words written on signs, I sang along with a one course menu of "Fresh Fried Riverside Soup from the Sound." Another sign announced "Summer Cooking Class" ½ price when you pay the full price for the Virginia Highland Festival of Distinctive Kitchen Tour. I did all the cooking in Norma Jean's kitchen full of her vanity, so a half-price summer cooking class didn't make the cut that summer sky blue afternoon.

Like I said, a kitchen tour was the last place I wanted to be, but my paper money pocket change money did all the talking. I just went along for the ride in my Mercedes with the top down. I was wearing a clean "wife beater" beneath a lightly starched, button-down white shirt and a nice summertime blazer. Light Scottish plaid against a Virginia summertime blue sky, my blazer blended out slightly more than it blended in.

I wasn't prepared to pay $40.00 worth of attention. Then, I saw the tour guide. She was a bombshell from a Greta Garbo,

Marilyn Monroe movie. I fell in and out of love so quickly I couldn't tell the difference. But the difference told me I was shellshocked back into remembering the night I met Miss Anna Everything (Anna Mae Sugarbaker) which was the same night I met Miss Norma Jean Smith. Miss Norma Jean beat me to punch. I smiled. That was my mistake.

So, it's no wonder, I stepped right up to the top of the tour and immediately forgot how long Norma jean's legs were and what color the tour guide's eyes were until the tour guide guided the seven of us, tour walkers, into the backdoor of the third house on the tour of distinctive kitchens in the Sweet Bay Area.

How we ricochet is a question that takes a room full of geniuses to halfway figure out. That day, I didn't even try to fathom why I bounced so solidly, finding myself in the middle of a magnificent moment. "15 Love," the physics of a tennis ball's topspin. I was painting the last inch of an inside tennis court corner. I was trying to defeat the fear of not believing Norma Jean still had my best interest tucked in the bosom of a wedding gown still hanging in the closet of the house where I used to park my Mercedes convertible.

Anyway, there we were in the kitchen of the third house on the tour. The seven of us, six left-over Southern Belles and me. The seven of us, six fifty-something homecoming queens and me. The seven of us, six middle of the weekday, champagne brunch ladies and me. The seven of us, six beach-read reading club members and me. The seven of us, six trophy wives, presented in full summertime fashion and me. The seven of us trading chats about Kentucky Derby hats and the names of Kentucky Derby horses. The seven of us looking for what each one of us needs in order to be able to say we don't need anything else.

What did the six of them think of the one of me, floating like a root beer float, is a question I forgot to ask myself. As prim and proper as those six ladies were, they were probably too prim and proper to answer in prim and proper Virginia blue daylight.

I could speculate, but you learn early in trailer park double wide life that speculation is an educated, uninformed determination made considering having nothing else to say about whatever happens to be the gossip-topic-of-conversation of the day. So, what they thought of me and what they thought of themselves were probably as different as they were the same.

Three cups of German hot wine even in the summertime make a certain kind of situation look at you differently even if you still must take everything in guesswork, measured out doses. I was still asking myself, "What am I doing in this woman's kitchen with six still-holding-on-to-be-primetime Barbie Dolls. Each of the six, pushing up dying tricks, wondering about the same thing, but from, decidedly, six different Virginia, upper upper-class angles and triangles. A Mozart moment, I needed at that moment. Mozart always answers his phone if he hears it ringing or not. You don't have to say anything. All you must do is listen to the way a trailer park wind blows a double wide breeze across a blue sky.

The tour guide, her name was Mrs. Elizabeth Birmingham Hamilton. And she made sure we remembered her name by placing her name on repeat mode. Mrs. Elizabeth Birmingham Hamilton was as theatrical as an off and on Broadway play if you ask me. By the end of scene 1, act 2, I was transfixed by the Southern gentility of leftover Confederate gray.

Most of what she said was tour-passing-time noise until she told us that we were in the kitchen of a Mrs. soon to be Miss Lesley Anne Downsberry. My nose was a bit stuffed up with confusion or delusion or both, but I could still smell the excitement of walking across the hickory hardwood floors of Mrs. soon to be Miss Lesley Anne Downsberry's kitchen.

I could hear jet airliners taking off from and landing in towns without airport runways just as easily as I could hear the pastel green, silver-grey and blue colors of words circling me like a circle of welcome wagons. Hallway walls recently painted, leading to Mrs. soon to be Miss Lesley Anne Downsberry's kitchen welcomed our company into the opened arms of British teacup royalty, Virginia style. Me, I was beyond bewildered by the tone in the sound of Lady Downsberry's name.

The eye of a hurricane is the stunning silence at the heart of a twister spinning me and my preoccupation with the sound of Lady's name, "Mrs. soon to be Miss Lesley Anne Downsberry." I could tell from the moment I met the sound of her name that she had a heart shaped like the smile of opening a gift. By the size and stack of her butcher block cutting board, I knew without a doubt that she was a woman with a manicured yard I would love to mow.

I could feel the cool, expensive granite countertop-blue warmness, 18 feet, asleep and snoring beneath the cold-colored blue cabinetry of Mrs. soon to be Miss Lesley Anne Downsberry's kitchen. I could taste the mid-afternoon sun shining through the mid-century, modern swing of her kitchen curtains. Then, I saw the details of the other side of her magic, her retro style, 1950s, mustard colored refrigerator.

For one long moment after another, my eyes wandered off and into the off-the-kitchen dining room of Mrs. soon to be Miss Leslie Anne Downsberry. Most people don't keep pictures of themselves in the dining room, but there she was looking out, mesmerizingly beautiful, looking out from a freshly polished, mahogany side table. Mrs. soon to be Miss Leslie Anne Downsberry, framed in an ornate, gold leaf frame. She was gracing her own dining room aesthetics with her own Hollywood, red carpet pose. Still, but not like a still-life, she was taking her own royal, sweet time, measuring the net worth of tourists and hometown visitors and me. Gracefully curated like an oil painting on the first floor of the Guggenheim Museum, she rearranged the tuck of my shirt with her eyes.

And just think, I only paid a $40.00 admission fee, four Abraham Lincolns and one Andrew Jackson. A Civil War

President Lincoln and a Battle of New Orleans President Jackson combined battlefield forces, flanking a Holy church collection plate. I was saved without knowing I had been saved. The soul saving smoothness of the front pocket exit felt like a fault line crossing a fault line. Strange how I never noticed that my broken heart was cracked in both directions. "That's what falling in love whispers to a broken heart," I spoke without saying in the foreign language of a retro style, 1950s, mustard colored refrigerator.

Three Women on the Seashore by Paul Gauguin graced one dining room wall. Directly across, not so graceful, Vincent Van Gogh, painting in slow brush strokes, *Mulberry Tree*, 1889. Nothing in the room centered itself around the temper flares of Paul Gauguin's attitude, but everything in the room, from fine bone China dinnerware to freshly polished sterling silver flatware complimented the off the dining room kitchen room retro-ness of Mrs. soon to be Miss Leslie Anne Downsberry's mustard yellow, retro 1956 refrigerator.

It wasn't until the last kitchen stop on the kitchen tour that I realized I was still at the third stop wondering what it would be like to put a six pack of beer in her refrigerator, wondering how long it would take to thaw out a steak from her refrigerator, wondering about the size of a ketchup bottle her refrigerator would accommodated, wondering which way was up and which way was down, wondering about the arithmetic of my upbringing divided into the mathematics of mustard colored love.

We snacked at the last stop on the tour, British biscuits with Earl or Lady Grey tea. But I wasn't hungry, I was still full of Mrs. soon to be Miss Lesley Anne Downsberry's cooking room and serving room aesthetics. The interior design of her two-room layout caused me to want to see the performing arts of her pots and pans and serving dishes. "What would it take to take a seat at her dinner table," I remember thinking out loud, so loud, I think the two of the ladies wearing Church Hill Downs horse racing hats heard me thinking. They were looking in the direction of me without looking at me, whispering brown sugar-coated words into the baking sweet smell of afternoon biscuits and tea. It was one of those moments when what you are thinking about becomes what you are smiling about.

The close of the tour of distinctive kitchens in the Sweet Bay area closed in on me as it closed out the Virginia sky-blue afternoon in the shape of a glued back-together broken plate. Street signs, stop lights and pigeons took careful notice of the bounce in my gait. I took off my blazer, fingered the hang-me-up-without-a hanger-loop, swung it across my left shoulder and walked away in the direction of moments not soon to be missed. Beautifully reflected in the eyes of Mrs. soon to be Miss Leslie Anne Downsberry was the next chapter of a story yet to be read by candlelight on top of a retro, 1950s style, mustard colored refrigerator.

Walking back to where I parked my sixteen-year-old Mersedes convertible, I was sixteen years old again, laughing and falling deeper. Love, I had fallen out of sight in a Lady's amazement. I was looking up into the Virginia sky blue when Mozart answered the phone. And this is what he told me, "Boy," Mozart said, "Don't try to stick no trailer park 6-pack of Bud light in that woman's refrigerator." In her voice you will not recognize, he said, "a 12-pack of Miller *High Life* the Champagne of Bottled Beer will make her say, 'Come here as clear as your first name.'"

The Perfect Game

(Where All Storms Are Perfect Storms)

Everybody knows she went to college on a lipstick scholarship, and the people had this and that to say about that. Everybody knows she quit cosmetology school without questions and the people had this and that to say about that. Making up art on the faces of country music mistresses, she made Nashville music sound good in the mirror for years. Without purpose, the people forgot what they said about that. But that was years ago. I wonder what faces she places in the stories she's making up now. I wonder if Rose Mary even bothers to make up a memory that remembers how many times I stole second base that spring of our senior year. I wonder if she remembers how many times I got caught looking at her.

This is the story of a perfect baseball game performed on a stage, perfect in time. The setting is perfect, a kaleidoscope of advertising signs and billboard signs wrapped around the outfield-homerun wall yelling can-I-sell-you-this, can-I- sell-you-that. Behind home plate, way up in the stands an old grey haired black man who calls himself, Mr. Ernest, we call him, Mr. Bojangles, is dancing up a game day hurricane without any signs of rain. Little children and big kids, running around the bases, trying to catch the wind, trying to touch home plate before the voice of God yells "Play ball." The infield is outfield until the summer-fan-noise level of baseball diamond shaped satisfaction is satisfied. The Bible said He sent his Son to save us, but we ain't ready to be saved, not quite yet.

The parking lot is a lot longer than an American-made pickup truck tailgate. In background, as far as the eye will let you see, Pepsi Cola signs and Coca Cola signs mad at each other because they can't occupy the same commercial space in South Carolina this afternoon.

Hot off the grill, grilled Ball Park brand hotdogs jazzed up in cheap-store chili. Cheap beer cans of Rolling Rock overly perfectly priced like Bud Lite and Miller Light, The Champagne of Ballpark Beer. Dollar Tree Cracker Jack box prizes still boxing a 1919 diamond shaped World Series ring that still wants to sing "Say it ain't so, Shoeless Joe, say it ain't so." Tacos and nachos and not enough cheese and too much cheese sell for the exact same price. A Mexico of habanero peppers adjust the thermostats of the game-time air. Everywhere, the afternoon colors of enjoyment, sunny-day-glow. Every detail, perfect as any prefect moment anyone in this town remembers. The weather lady said the weather would be Saturday-afternoon perfect. And she was perfectly right.

Almost every bleacher seat in the house, taken or mistaken to be taken. The crowd, a perfect standing ovation, cheering for the hometown team to take the field. Brothers and mothers, farmers, and daughters basking in the sunbeams of Beansville. A Saltlife, low country breeze blowing the smell of somebody frying fish. The catch of the day was actually caught today. Game time day drunk anticipation is the perfect home field advantage as long as you know that the art of stealing second base is an exact science, especially when you get caught looking, multiplying a miscalculation

I don't know if I memorized my multiplication tables when I was in the third grade or when I was in the fifth grade. Or maybe it was that leap year when the first day of summer forgot to come on time for opening day baseball. That may very well be as long as you know there's only one ordinary number between 3 and 5. As far back as I can remember, low tide and high tide, waves of baseball voices kept me running bases from sometime in May until the very last dog day of August baseball year. All I know for sure is learning my multiplication table must have taken an awful long time based on how much red lipstick and red rouge Rose Mary's mother allowed Rose Mary to wear to the ninth-grade school dance.

As hard as I tried to get on base every time I stepped up to the plate, I was unable to multiply why Rose Mary turned me down every time I asked her to dance. What is the arithmetic answer when 5 "May I have this dance" is multiplied by 5 "No, I don't think so"s. Dejected, in love, madly, with the smile of red painted lips, I walked away 25 times, it seems. But that can't be right. Or who knows when a calculator can't count from 1 to 10 without getting crossed up in red. It was late April, a nice feeling Thursday night. You know the kind of night that makes you want to stay up all night. And I didn't plan on going to school the next day, anyway. The next day was my fifteenth birthday, just as forgettable as my fourteenth. But my thirteenth, I remember without thinking. I was thirteen years and one hundred and two days old when Rose Mary's mother first let Rose Mary wear red lipstick and rouge to homeroom class. I can still see the 1st period frown on Miss Purdy's pretty face.

Sixteen years and two months later, sometimes still, I can feel the rowing and raging pull of color, Rose Mary's red rouge, her lipstick when I think about those junior high school days. Yes, I know, my locker was across the hallway from hers. And yes, it's true she let me pick up a book she dropped a time or two. And oh yeah, she let me sit beside her on the school bus a couple of times, and one time she asked me if I thought Miss Purdy was pretty and I said I think so. Oh yeah, and there was that time she let me tie her tennis shoe because the strings were too long for her long teenage legs. Rose Mary's legs, so beautiful that angels who decided not to go to Heaven right away were probably jealous.

But I still don't know why Rose Mary said "no" every time I asked her to dance. I know her mother took her to church every Sunday and sometimes on Wednesday nights, so maybe it was Jesus or Joseph, Jesus's stepdad, who told Rose Mary not to dance with me. But how can that be without some farther explanation?

Years later, I can, now, do the mathematical explanation of my 3 married "lifes" and arrive at some kind of loose-end conclusion. One- and one-half marriages multiplied by 2 rented tuxedos equals 3 divorces. Each divorce straight, no chaser, on the rocks from start to finish. My fault, probably. I know I'm no easy problem to solve. My mother said 3 blessings blessed when I was born, thanks Mom, but like so many relationships and sailboats, I just sail on until I sink in a sea of what's left over. Like so many people, my remainders have always been bigger numbers than the honest answer to the simplest long division problem and that's a problem on any planet in the universe except Neptune, my next stop. Yard sale, everything must go, moving to Neptune.

Neptune, where arithmetic mistakes apply themselves equally in love and in war. I tried to love the hurricane eyes between battle zones, I really did. Only my middle wife loved me like no other, but she was split in half, straight down the middle. The first half of my middle marriage, I was still in love with my first wife, so I thought. The second half of my middle marriage, I was in love with my third wife to be, so I thought. So I, now, think not twice but 3 times before concluding anything about me and my love of whoever and whatever forever.

"Take another shot of that Tennessee whiskey," straight no chaser chased me away 3 times. And I always left "leaving," always already packed. The trajectory of touring, I always had a ball game to play. Even during off-season, I was always ready to sing "that song," John Fogerty singing in the center of a Carolina cornfield that 1985 summertime song, "Put me in coach, I'm ready to play today. Look at me, I can be centerfield."

Today looks back at me looking back at myself and my world between base lines and foul balls. I see my clothes thrown on the sidewalks of 3 small towns without enough concrete to make them cities. Running away from love when you think you are running toward love is an art no one wants to master. But I'm a master of a lot of things I don't want to be. I'm still running, every chance I get, outside the base path. Stealing love is not like stealing second base. Stealing love is more like stealing fruit from a curbside fruit stand. You intended to pay, you really did, but you forgot that the price of love is always overpriced like ballpark beer. So, your broken heart must remain broken because you are broke. Way before I could afford not to, I always carried a pocket full of pocket change in case I needed to dry my life out one night at some random laundry mat.

I play center field for the Watchouts; I make pretty good money. Over the course of a Holy matrimony of up and down years, I've paid and I've paid and I've paid. I was always afraid to want any kids. And maybe that was good because I lost 3 houses in one hurricane. 3 times that same named hurricane with those hypnotizing eyes hypnotized me into signing, then assigning a higher interest rate to an already paid-off mortgage. Each wife in my life walked away with a 3-bath, 3-bedroom house. It's funny, it's Sunday morning newspaper cartoon funny, but being married to me, 3 judges and 3 juries decided, is like the tag and miss of a left-handed baseball glove worn on the wrong fist full of dollar bills. Enough is enough to smile about some days, and some other days it's nowhere near where you would think it would be. A smile on an evil woman's face has always fascinated me. In many ways, that's how I ended up here.

Today is in the middle of a cracked-up firecracker baseball

season. I'm in the batter's box, a 4 ft by 6ft rectangle on either side of home plate. I'm multiplying again. Like walking beneath a shadow, from the on-deck circle, I walked beneath a hail of boos. They don't like us. We don't like them. An all-out all-American rivalry, some say. The Lookouts are playing us, the Watchouts. We have home field advantage, but they are leading, 1 run to none. The home teams bats last and this is it. It's the bottom of the 9th inning of an almost perfect game.

It's prime time television time. I'm a switch hitter. I bat left-handed when the opposing pitcher is throwing right-handed. I bat right-handed when the opposing pitcher is throwing left-handed. It's interleague play. I am now batting in the nine-spot in the bottom of the ninth inning. There are two 2 outs. The crowd is chanting and re-singing the lyrics of that tin Pan alley, seventh inning stretch song, "Take me out to the ball game…buy me some peanuts and cracker jack." The whole baseball world is one out away from a perfect game. Let me explain, in baseball there are 9 innings and 3 outs per inning. A perfect game is 9 times 3 equals 27 straight outs without any batter reaching first base. 27 batters up, 27 batters sat right back down.

After having studied the Lookout rotations of an impending shutout, I am borderline, and baseline perplexed. Yes, it's the Holy, sacred bottom of the 9th inning. Batter number 25 grounded out, hung his head, walked back to the dugout, and disappeared into baseball game day dust. Batter number 26 flied out to right, hung his head, walked back to the dugout, and disappeared too. I'm batter number 27, hoping not to just disappear in some kind of thin dust bowl. The dirt floor of the batter's box is adjusting and readjusting my cleats for me. I am not moving at all on my own. My 32oz. Louisville, Kentucky keeps dancing on its own, own accord. In the stands, in every direction, drama women, drama men, drama boys, drama girls and drama little kids with no idea why, all dramatize the anticipation of a perfect game. The umpire sweeps home plate clean with a handheld size broom, puts it back into his back pocket and pulls his face mask down over his face.

Everywhere in the air, fat ladies are getting ready to sing Glory Hallelujah. The game-time announcer is announcing my name, Joe so 'n' so. 60 feet and 6 inches away, I'm looking at how a Lookout pitcher's hand grips the seams of a baseball. I'm trying to figure out the multiplied relationship between distance and velocity, between time and space, between earth and Neptune.

Strike one. A 97 mile an hour fastball with big boobs and looking glass eyes, I swing, I miss and fall in and out of love at the same time. Her name was Daisy Mae, and she was wearing Daisy Dukes. It was at a cock fight where we met in the backside of backwoods Georgia. I can't tell you what I was doing there except I got lost and took a wrong turn on purpose because I didn't want to go where I was going. Now, that's another story I don't feel like telling, but I will tell you this. She was my first marriage. The marriage lasted for as long as it lasted. She was the sweetest girl I've ever met in my life, but I've always been scared of sweet Southern women. She was strike one with a wind speed of reasons.

Strike two. Mary Sue looked like a strike two before the pitch left the pitcher's hand. And then from out of nowhere comes a breaking ball, 82 miles per hour slow. A two-seamer slow-breaking that catches me looking into Mary Sue's eyes and not looking at the way a breaking ball drops out of sight just before reaching wherever it reaches. I swing, I miss the moment our drunk eyes locked like two high school hallway lockers. She was five years older than me. She was an art teacher, and I was an art student studying the art of knocking the cover off of a baseball. I got lost in her blue eyes; we got married behind the church. It was an uphill marriage made in Heaven that never made it out of the courthouse except on paper. You know what they say about paper money. Strike two, one strike to go.

My third wife was born a "strike three call" so, I don't need to tell you how beautifully crazy she was. She was a circuit court judge, so I won't mention how many courts-appointed attorneys she appointed from her short-skirt-side of a county courthouse bench. And I'm not going to tell you what she did before she decided to appoint herself as her own attorney in case #17773, She vs Me. And you probably already know an 18-carat diamond ring and a 9-inning baseball game diamond are about the same size if you know your multiplication table.

I loved that circuit court judge like a criminal, yes I loved her like I was getting ready to steal a car but she didn't like ironing boards and vacuum cleaners and washing clothes and watching the percolating smell of coffee brewing today on this pitcher's mound, a perfect storm, a perfect game.

And then the cheering crowd, dead pan still. So quiet now, you can hear freeway traffic rushing by, going wherever rushing traffic goes on perfect Saturday afternoons. The talking heads tongue-tied in loose knots, announcing nothing at the moment. All is quiet on both sides of Lake Anticipation. The longest moment of the year is speechless.

Dug in to win, both dugouts hold their collective breath. The hotdog man and the peanuts girl pose in pause mode. An incoming plane seems to stop in midair. The beer-selling boys have run out of beer by mistake. The ballboy has ants in his pants but dares to dance. Right field and left field shift right, then shift left. Centerfield stays dead center. The third base coach has run out of chewing gum. The catcher keeps changing signs of an earlier time. The pitcher keeps shaking each sign off. The umpire keeps adjusting the angle of his across-home-plate view. The manager keeps spitting sunflower seed hulls into an anxious pile. Time is just about to stop ticking.

Into the artistry of his windup motion, the pitcher throws with the high leg kick of yesteryears. The left leg arches toward the sky, his left cleat reaching higher than the bill of his cap. Then here comes the night, the fire, the blaze hurling through a clear haze, another 97 miles an hour fastball zipping toward home plate. Do I swing, do I swing, do I...? I swing, I miss. Strike three. Laughters of lava, voices of volcanos erupt.

At first, I couldn't figure it out, but at last I got the answer right. The time and distance back to the dugout turns out to be the loudest, longest, loneliest walk I have ever taken. Time forgot how not to be slow. I know what a head full of fog feels like, but I've not been this fogged-in since I was a kid growing up in San Francisco. "Hey joe."

It's funny how a recognized voice sounds foreign coming from an unexpected time of day. "Hey Joe." Above the noise level of how and why, the star of the story's soft whisper is loud enough to find me. There above the home team dugout, in the stands, in the first row, a red lipstick face from sixteen years ago hurls her seven words, easily, down upon me cool as a July rainstorm, most often, refuses to be. The long, hot, rainy dog days of August are not over, not quite yet. I do not, honestly, know what to say, so I say, "How many years would it take us if we to walk to Neptune. "

The Great Train Robbery

The November morning was as clear blue as Alabama skies get, the one in Jackson's head and the one above Jackson's head looking down upon the scene of the mistake. At the front edge of Jackson's mind was a photograph of Anna dancing. At the other edge was another photograph of Anna dancing. In-between images of the dance, solid, the methodical dissection of how to plan a mistake.

Years later, the mistake, white as two glasses of expensive white wine. Actually, it was one of the last remaining candle-lit evenings of 1977. It was the night before Christmas. Jackson and his wife, Anna, had been celebrating for a full month. Jackson had been named full partner. The sign out front of the firm reads Taylor, Faulkner, Stevenson and Sullivan. Jackson had finally made it to the summit of Good Barrister Mountain Row. Jackson Dempsey Sullivan was now a big-time lawyer in a small-time Alabama town where everybody knows who will do what and when. Jackson's hometown, a sunny-side-of-the-street town where everybody knows without knowing the scientific strategy of how and why Jackson Dempsey Sullivan, Esquire came to be.

Jackson's first big case in his new role was just seventeen days away, when he remembered the last time that he dreamed of the vivid details of how his name came to be printed on the front side of a handsome, handmade designed sign. A street-side big sign planted in celebration of one of the most prestigious Law

Firms in Greene County, Alabama graced the lowest level of the cityscape.

Ironically or incidentally or both, the over the top, oversized Taylor, Faulkner, Stevenson and Sullivan sign planted itself in a fertile city-field located, approximately, fourteen and one-half city blocks northwest of where Jackson Dempsey Sullivan grew up, throwing footballs up and down a quiet street. The seventeen streets between the placement of the sign and the Negro street corners of Negro preoccupations with racial tension almost made the placement of the Taylor, Faulkner, Stevenson and Sullivan sign a historical marker. Only Jackson delighted in the fact that the sign located itself just three blocks over from where Sears Roebuck used to be before Sears Roebuck moved to the mall.

Jackson Dempsey Sullivan's story is the story of the history of the Year of Our Lord, 1968. 1968, the Chinese Year of the clever-hearted Monkey. 1968, the year Jackson Dempsey Sullivan fell in love with Miss Anna Belle Mansfield.

Moments of the drama, 1968, the year of The Great Train Robbery of 1903, revised.

1968, the year Elvis' Comeback Special aired on NBC. 1968, the year Martin Luther King Jr. was assassinated on the balcony of the Lorraine Motel in Memphis, Tennessee. 1968, the year Robert Francis Kennedy was assassinated at the Ambassador Hotel ballroom in Los Angeles after giving a speech. 1968, the summer of the Olympic Stadium-Mexico City medal ceremony Black Power Salute. 1968, the year of John Carlos and Tommie Smith, holding up the whole African American world for a moment, decided not to smile for the camera.

1968, the year of twisting the night away, the year of a whole lot of shaking going on, the year of black velvet slow Southern style night music, the year of a Yellow People War, the year of a gold and a silver, Black Power fist touching the sky over Olympic City, the year of two deadly target practice sessions that spilled two months (April and June) of blood onto the already deadly soiled calendar pages of 365 ¼ mean spirited-rumored days.

1968, Jackson was on the downside of his junior year. Jackson was 18 years old, when he got draft notice announcement for his Uncle Sam. His sister, Caroline, who graduated with the class of 1967 had signed up for the Navy and was waiting and still working at Sears Roebuck. But, mostly, Caroline was still preoccupied with getting back at or getting away from the boy who didn't ask her to senior prom. Caroline Anne just couldn't get over Mason (Ran the Man) Taylor going to the senior prom with "that" Homecoming Queen. Every morning, for a while afterwards, when Caroline Anne Sullivan looked in the mirror, she quietly, softly said to her reflection, "I'm way prettier than that 'thing.'"

Marie Catherine Carpenter, the Ridgemont High School Homecoming Queen of 1967, was the classic girl next door in, at a minimum, two ways. She had a head full of platinum blonde hair. She had Carolina blue eyes that hinted at a soft shade of green. She had a figure that could figure out the hardest math problem in the book. All the boys and male teachers took her algebraic measurements every time Marie Catherine Carpenter decided to wiggle her hips. Her legs, longer than a long division problem on a timed Arithmetic test.

Queen Marie Catherine's turn-of-the-19th century, Italian Baroque looking house was three door-knocks down from the house that Caroline and Jackson's daddy inherited from his father. Caroline and Jackson's partly brick, one-story, fifties ranch style, proudly situated in the middle of the block, was always good to the neighborhood kids. An even house on an even street, 1452 Squirrel Run Trail was an address that the U. S. Postal Service didn't care much for because Caroline and Jackson's mother was a catalog and magazine queen. The Sears Roebuck annual catalog was on the top shelf of magazine racks of catalog magazines in the corners of Caroline and Jackson's living room and fireplace room. Like all the boys Jackson knew and probably the ones Jackson did not know, his favorite section of the Sears Roebuck catalog was the excitement of the women's underwear pages. His second favorite was the hunting rifles, and the fly fishing rods pages.

At the turn of the century, Caroline and Jackson's grandparents came to America from Ireland as immigrants. They first settled in Pittsburgh, Pennsylvania. They faced the "Dish Washers Needed, Irish Need Not Apply" sign. Still, their grandfather got a job working in the steel industry and their grandmother ironed other people's laundry. They lived a "make ends meet" life for a decade or so before they moved to a small town outside of Montevallo, Alabama. There, their grandfather got work in the coal mining industry.

Caroline and Jackson's parents, William Dempsey Sullivan and Marilyn Murphy Sullivan, established themselves as lower middle class community pillars in the same Alabama small town. Dempsey Sullivan worked at the town's chemical factory and Marilyn Murphy Sullivan taught kindergarten and sold cakes and pies to an established ring of neighbors on the weekend before Christmas and Thanksgiving and sometimes on the Saturday before Mother's Day. Together, they made enough to, solidly, raise their two children. Caroline and Jackson's upbringing was typical 3rd generation Irish Catholic American. The family went to mass every Sunday morning and sunrise service every Easter.

Mr. and Mrs. William Dempsey Sullivan's circle of acquaintances and friends was mostly an Irish Catholic circle with a fair number of Baptist, Methodist and Presbyterian exceptions. Dempsey Sullivan loved cars to a fault. He loved tinkering with them, fixing them up. Jackson spent many Saturday mornings washing and polishing his daddy's cars. When he was old enough, Jackson's daddy taught Jackson how to drive. Jackson's daddy didn't teach Caroline, she took Driver's Education classes her junior year. Mr. Dempsey always tried to keep a pretty, good running car parked in the Sullivan driveway. Ford or Chevrolet, Oldsmobile or Dodge Rambler, it didn't really matter as long as his automobile looked like it was the sleekish on the block, as long as it was the envy of the people who drove up and down Squirrel Run Trail Street.

Dempsey Sullivan had his peculiarities and particularities. His supper always had to be on time. He went to bed at the same time every night, even on weekends. He got up at the same time every morning and he almost always had Mrs. Sullivan pack two baloney sandwiches in his lunch pail, one with mustard and one with mayonnaise. He loved the routine nature of things almost as much as he loved his wife, his high school sweetheart. Mrs. Sullivan was a standard, everyday homemaker. A picture of a Southern woman wearing an apron was Marilyn's standard in-the-kitchen pose.

When Marilyn was too young to know how to tie her shoes, her mother was teaching Marilyn how to sew. And she could sew by hand like a sewing machine. She wasn't the least bit intimidated by threading needles or the colors of thread that don't really match the patterns of whatever she was matching. Mr. Dempsey bought his wife a Singer sewing machine for Mother's Day one year. From then on, she made more floral print and plaid print dresses for herself than she could ever wear to church, PTA meetings, ladies' meetings and garden club get-togethers.

Marilyn Murphy Sullivan tried, but Caroline Anne Sullivan would have none of her mother's old fashion-ness. Caroline Anne Sullivan, always fashion-forward watching and looking for the latest fashion trend. Caroline Anne and her schoolgirl friends loved to spend Saturdays walking up and down window-shopping streets. For days before purchase, they took their time deciding. Caroline Anne and her schoolgirl friends preferred to take their sweet time figuring out fashion trends by studying their own reflections in department store dressing room's mirrors.

1968, the year of cotton blend and polyester miniskirts. Miniskirts that young girls and older women, including Caroline and her schoolgirl friends, styled in the face of all who opposed made the front cover page of Look and Life magazine. The miniskirts styling up and down the hallways of Ridgemont High School were just as short as miniskirts anywhere else on the short hem spectrum. In 1968, it was fashion-worthy understood and misunderstood that season made no difference. During fall, winter, spring and summer in small towns and cities everywhere, showing more high-thigh than necessary was all the rage.

1968, the year somebody federally forced somebody to integrate Ridgemont High School. 1968, the year somebody struck a match, didn't close cover before striking and lit the fuse of a firecracker box full of race riots. 1968, the year somebody tossed the flames in every direction in America. 1968 was when it all started, but 1968 was not the beginning.

The Great Robbery, a silent movie made in 1903, as far Jackson could tell, was the very beginning of how the story ends. Cowboy movies and cartoons and "Who dun it" television programs carved a highway through Jackson's heart. What and who travelled those roads, Jackson could only speculate. All he knew was that he loved the black and white courtroom drama of Public Defender, Perry Mason. When he was 16 years old, Jackson decided he wanted to be a master criminal defense attorney, handling the most difficult cases in support of the innocent. Jackson's father was always on the side of the outlaw. Jackson's father always said that outlaws had proper cause to be outlaws.

As a kid he often found himself fascinated by cops and robbers television shows. Before he knew the meaning of the word, mitigate, he played cartoon court without a jury or judge. He associated the word lawyer with winning every cartoon case. So, what turned out to be the wrong side of the table to be eating from with a fork in the wrong hand grew up to be Jackson's ambitious advantage. "All good lawyers are left-handed,"

Jackson couldn't remember which cartoon episode told him that. "And you're right-handed," Jackson remembers exactly who told him that. So little Jackson learned that in a sideways way, cowboy movies and cartoons are more real than people give them credit for being.

As little as Jackson was, watching The Great Train Robbery with his drinking-beer father sitting on the couch beside him, Jackson remembers two bandits breaking into a telegraph office, forcing the operator to stop the train, then a gang of outlaws holdup and rob the steam train, then flee across mountainous terrain. A silent movie, as little as Jackson was, he wondered why the shoot 'em ups, the blow 'em ups, and the kill 'em ups scenes did not make a single television screen sound.

The television didn't talk movie-night talk. He couldn't read the words quick enough before the words changed scenes and scenarios. But he was cinematically impressed and hijacked by the swiftness, exactness and excitement of the gangster-outlaw-bandit movement. Jackson worshipped what he couldn't hear to the point that his life from the time he was a little boy has been sealed in a silent picture show train robbery where the characters move their lips, but no sound comes out of their mouths.

1968, the year Jackson got his draft notice in the mail. The return address said Uncle Sam Wants You. It was on the dining room table stuck between a Harper's Bazaar magazine and a Sears Roebuck catalog. 18 years old, going into his senior year, Jackson was a year older than most of his senior classmates. He was held back in 3rd grade because he missed too many school days because he was sick with something no one was ever able to decide. He went down to the Draft Board, but didn't have to report for duty because his sister, Caroline had already joined the Navy." The Draft Board man told Jackson that the U. S. Military had a policy against having siblings serving at the same time unless they, both, volunteered.

Jackson had already started to imagine his last name,

SULLIVAN sown across the heart of an Army green shirt that would have no problem matching army green pants tucked into the shine of Amry black boots. In the back of his mind, he had been looking forward to busting targets with an M-16. But when, in his mind, target practice traded places with the faces of yellow people, Jackson's forward look stopped looking forward. He placed his visions of weapons back into holsters and set his sights on becoming an outlaw lawyer, shooting down criminal cases.

1968, the year President Lyndon Baines Johnson sent 10,000 troops to Vietnam. 1968, the year the North Vietnamese launched the Tet Offensive, the largest offensive of the war. 1968, the year Apollo 8 showed the world, for the first time, the far side of the moon.

1968, the 12th of August, a dry, hot Alabama day, 107 "Black is Beautiful" faces came to decorate the way a school year unfolds in heated times. They added a rich textured, colored complexion to the way the white kids walked up the stairs and down the racist-ly noisy hallways of Ridgemont High and Ridgemont Elementary. Most students seemed coolly content and happy for the most part, but Former Governor George Wallace was not happy at all about how rapidly the tides of the times were changing. All of this was according to radio, television and newspaper news. Former Governor George Wallace was too busy trying to "outnigger" his way to the top of his next ambition, the President of the United States.

1968, the year George Corley Wallace, Jr. threw his hat into the presidential ring of riots and fire. 1968, the year Richard Milhous Nixon decide to run for president against the brother of his 1960 defeat. 1968, the year Jackson Dempsey Sullivan started hanging out with Screaming Tree and Bird. Jokingly, Jackson would call his new friends like they were old buddies, "Red Tree and Black Bird." Before Jackson Dempsey Sullivan met David Screaming Tree and Wayne Bird Jr., Jackson's life was a one note song. Conversations with Tree and Bird extended

Jackson's musical vocabulary, and he started to hear notes before they were played.

Screaming Tree, everybody called him Tree, was a tall, Abraham Lincoln lanky fellow. David Screaming Tree was his real name as it was written in his homeroom teacher's roll book. Tree said he was an Alabama Creek Indian; said he didn't have any parents. When Jackson asked, "Then, man, where did you come from?" Tree said he came from somewhere around Red River, Arkansas on a trout fishing boat when he was too little to remember to know not to play "Catch me if you can" with black bears.

Tree was the definition of a stereotype, a buck, brave and red with long black hair. Tree had warrior-brown eyes. Most people didn't want to even think about tangling with Tree. Tree could climb myself. That boy was agile as a red ballet dancer. Jackson loved talking to Tree because Tree always talked a mouth full of nonsense that ended up making perfect sense. Tree said, "You grab 'em by the shoulders and you spin 'em around and around 'til they are vertigo, convoluted and confused, then you show 'em which way is up, and which way is down, then you turn the directions upside down." Jackson put that note in his shirt pocket the first time and the second time he heard it coming from the Native American quietness of that pony boy's mouth. David Screaming Tree could ride an Appaloosa like a silent western picture show, dancing across the "Bad Lands," chasing bad guys on bad weather days, jumping over tumble weeds without making a sound. Outlaws chasing outlaws. Each trying to be the baddest outlaw in the "Bad Lands."

Bird had stubborn hair that got tired of trying to be an afro. The afro pick Bird carried in his back pocket was too big for his head. Bird played saxophone magic like the famous Charlie "Bird" Parker. That's why he referred to himself in third person, "Bird gonna break the bank." It took almost a year before Jackson figured out the alliteration in the way Bird smiled every time Bird let his saxophone ask, "Who's in the audience tonight." Most of the other students called him Bird to his face, but some called him "Nigger Bird" when he wasn't looking.

Bird was a single-parent Bird. Before somebody decided to let him attend a white high school and before he met Jackson and Tree and before his mama moved them out of a red brick housing project home, Bird lived a life of thunder and pounding rain. Red brick project life where every kid, growing up, is a government "project," is how Bird described it with his saxophone. The first time the three met, they were standing in a triangle by mistake. The mistake that led the three of them to the courtyard was honest. Each one looking for each other without knowing that was the case.

Bird told Jackson and Tree that the only white people who dared to venture into his Negro red brick projects were policemen and Jewish "rent to own" furniture salesmen. "Everybody I know sleeps on a barrowed bed," Bird told the story of everything, "Everybody I know is caught up in the commercial commotions of a 'Fifteen Dollars a Week-for the rest of your life' everyday- holiday furniture sale." Bird didn't talk much. Bird just blew the red brick projects of words out of the end of his saxophone. Smoothly, Bird's words drifted up and out onto courtyards of cleared up confusion.

Jackson Dempsey Sullivan was named after the great Irish American boxer, Jack Dempsey. William Harrison "Jack" Dempsey, nicknamed Kid Blackie, was an American professional boxer. Jack Dempsey was a cultural icon of the 1920's. Jackson's father loved Jack Dempsey as much as he loved the smell of a brand-new Chevrolet. And apparently, he loved his brand-new baby boy, Jackson to name him after an Irish. Although Jackson's father was a slow-to-the-to-draw daddy, like Jack Dempsey, Jackson Dempsey Sullivan had hands fast enough to catch the Negro groove of what Bird was talking about with his horn. Tree didn't talk much either, but he told the history of

Native American life with his silence. Without saying one word, both Tree and Bird told Jackson to "Listen only to that which listens to you."

Six months before the night of the thunderstorm without thunder, Jackson's father had been dead Six months in the other direction. He had been driving to work, not late because he was so on-time routine, when a bump in the road spilled his coffee in his lap. The top was not screwed tight. It wasn't that hot, but he looked down too long. Five days later, William Dempsey Sullivan was buried in the Alabama heat of a Thursday afternoon. His father had no life insurance policy. How could he now go to college, not to mention law school? "The sky that had been so wide open and blue has now folded up on you," Jackson heard himself say to himself, repeatedly, that night until he fell asleep dreaming of a Jack Dempsey defeat.

Tyrone, a six-foot, fleet-footed fox of a boy, dark brown-black and beautiful with a hint of gold in his appearance. "Tyrone has royal African roots," was Jackson's initial observation. All the white girls loved Tyrone, but 1968 was not kind to that kind of acknowledgement in black and white photography. So, every picture in the Ridgemont High School year book of 1968 was taken in technicolor or not taken at all.

So even after Jackson climbed out of the hole by standing on the shoulders of Tree, even after teaching himself the meaning of the reach of blues lyrics dancing out of the mouth of Bird's sax, Jackson, still, kept his ambition to go to law school in his back pocket. His father had been the money behind Jackson's dream. What would he do now to make two stubborn ends meet. It wasn't until the day Tree and Bird introduced Jackson to the tornadic winds of Romell Tyrone Tucker that Jackson's sky opened back up. That day in the Ridgemont High School hallway, Tyrone blew the wind back into Jackson's sail with six words, "Smooth criminals make the best lawyers."

Whether it was ironic or Devine or the simultaneity of the

two, there it was, laying on the kitchen counter. Caroline came home that night with an extra set of keys. When Jackson inquired, Caroline told him that they were Sears Roebuck Jewelry counter keys. The hardware store closes at 9:00, Jackson thought out loud. Jackson made it there at 8:55.

Caroline had inadvertently brought the jewelry counter key home when it should have been left in its secret place behind the jewelry counter. That night Caroline was working behind the cosmetic counter, her regular place, which was just across the way from the jewelry counter when she noticed a woman that needed assistance in jewelry. The woman waited and waited. Where is everybody, Caroline thought. Caroline called her manager, and her manager, her manager didn't answer, so Caroline did what a good salesperson should do. It was a few minutes before closing time. Caroline knew the jewelry counter code. Caroline had a head for numbers. One day Miss Sally came to work without her glasses and Caroline had to punch in the numbers, 732777532825, because Miss Sally couldn't get the jewelry counter gate to swing open wide enough to accommodate her rather large hips.

Caroline was an early packer. Her suitcases were already packed, sitting by the door a full fortnight before she was scheduled to ship off to the Navy. Caroline's premature packed luggage corresponded with her Sears Roebuck two-week notice. Mrs. Sullivan complained, but Caroline's suitcases were too madly in love with getting ready to go join the Navy.

Jupiter Smith was the smartest student in Caroline's graduating class, but he was too black to be voted valedictorian. Jupiter came to Ridgemont High School the year before integration. Jupiter was Tyrone's cousin, and the reason Tyrone moved from Birmingham to finish high school. Before Tyrone moved from Birmingham, he worked at, according to him, The Birmingham, Alabama Mafia Headquarters Spaghetti Restaurant. Every weekday morning, men in dark suits conducted breakfast meeting over coffee at back tables. Fried spaghetti with meatballs with a fried egg on top was listed at the top of a first-class breakfast menu. Tyrone paid close attention and moved up in the ranks to the point that he knew the details of exactly what was going on in the Drive-Around-Back Room. The Drive-Around-Back Room had one rule, "You don't ask any questions, no questions will be asked." Certain policemen came in for lunch a couple times a month. They always ate for free. They always left carrying more than they entered carrying. Tyrone was an inside employee. They paid Tyrone under the table and on top of the table, quite handsomely, because Tyrone could recite, verbatim, the whole inside makeup of a true crime story.

Jackson unfolded his true crime story before refolding it into the strides of his walk away from the center of the Drive-Around-Back-Room. He took the longest route of two long routes thinking about the courtroom drama of the Drive-Around courtroom in the back of a spaghetti house restaurant that he was walking away from. A scene, perhaps, from a stage play: An un-honorable judge and a 12-man jury behind the dark glasses of one man wearing a dark suit. No "All rise" moment, no call your next witness, no objections, no counter claims, no cross-examination, no circumstantial evidence, no insufficient evidence, no closing argument.

Walking away from one life into the unknowns of another, the walking weight of the verdict, a backpack full of 100-dollar bills, was heavier than Jackson had imagined the night he went to the hardware store just in time to make a copy of Caroline's mistaken Sears Roebuck jewelry counter key.

Walking, he thought about how he got Caroline to tell him the layout of the store's cameras, over the cash registers, exit/entrance doors and ironically not over the jewelry counter. He thought about how he got Caroline to give him the code, 732777532825, without Caroline realizing she was giving her brother the script for The Great Robbery. He thought about his mother and where he told her he would be spending the night that night. He thought about changing clothes in his car, left parked a block from the bus stop and what seemed like thirty blocks away from Sears Roebuck. He thought about Anna.

Talking to himself, Jackson congratulated Tree, Bird and Tyrone, contributors to a night without a moon. They had no idea of the parts they played in Jackson's solo, theatrical production of The Great Train Robbery. Walking at the pace of slow contemplation, Jackson thought about the city bus ride to Sears Roebuck that stopped too many nervous times. Bus riders seemed to pay little attention to Jackson that night. He laughed about how well his sister's long dress was a prefect disguise when paired with the size 12 black flats, pleather shoes it took him forever to convince the Butler Shoes saleslady he was buying for his wife.

Cars and taxis drove by. Traffic stop-lights warned him to wait. High heels crowded the sidewalks of the moment. Jackson studied the movement and magic of ladies' shoes. Businessmen, briefcases, business suits and neck ties went as fast as they came to Jackson's attention. He thought about his sister Caroline's oversized purse and the tote bag he carried, quietly, like a rich woman on the night in question. He smiled about the blonde wig he wore over his long blond hair. He thought about the Halloween mask he wore at the scene of the crime. He thought about the tight fit of latex gloves. He thought about what Tyrone told him before he, himself, knew the plot to the play "Smooth criminals make the best lawyers" because they always work solo. Solo because there are questions. The one that knows who, when and what is the only one that knows. He thought about the 30 minutes judge and jury deliberation, the longest 30 minutes of his life. He thought about the nubs of his bitten down fingernails. He thought about his ring finger. He thought about Anna.

He thought about the timing of the night of the crime. The next morning, Sears would be opening at 6am, the opening bell of a Day Break, sunrise, Sale. He thought about entering the store, unannounced, just before Sears Roebuck's 11pm Holiday closing time, making his way upstairs to the bedding section, then sliding in place under a queen-size bed in the corner of the bedroom showroom. He thought about the cool patience of the wait before and the wait afterwards; hours on one side of midnight are longer than hours on the other side of midnight. He thought about what he was thinking about, looking up into cloudy sky of a queen size box spring.

He thought about the mannequin ghosts watching him punch in 732777532825. He thought about how easily the below-the-counter jewelry drawers did exactly what the hardware store key told them to do. He thought about how he didn't touch the jewelry that was case-customer displayed. He knew that The Great Train Robbery would only be discovered when Miss Sally or her help saw that the jewelry boxes in the drawers were empty boxes. He thought about how methodically the oversized purse and the tote bag filled themselves with diamond rings, gold necklaces, diamond laced tennis bracelets, gold and bronze wedding bands, gold and sterling silver earrings, gemstones and gold-plated watches. He thought about the number of times he looked up to see if the mannequin ghosts were still watching and finally watched him place the tote bag into a Sears Roebuck shopping bag.

He thought about how he didn't account for having to pee under a queen-size bed. He thought about waiting 30 minutes after the sunrise opening, so he could exit with the customers who had waited in line the longest and carried the biggest Sears Roebuck shopping bags out to a crowded parking lot. He thought how the sun refused to look at him that partly cloudy morning and about how the city bus was waiting on him by the time he made it to the bus stop. He thought about how the mostly black bus riders admired the weight of his Sears Roebuck shopping bag.

Walking at a quicker pace, Jackson thought about the distance between his thoughts and the Birmingham Greyhound bus station sign. When he reached the doorsteps of the sign, he thought about the color of the sky upon his arrival at 19th Street North, Birmingham, Alabama. He thought about his mother's sewing machine. He thought about his sister's Navy uniform, and he thought about his father's Irish-American smile. His father had left Jackson with the stability of looking at the world through the lens of hope, but he didn't leave Jackson a way out of becoming a routine person working a routine job. He thought about the years his father worked, only to end up with nothing to, now, speak kindly of.

The Birmingham Greyhound bus station sign made Jackson think about Bird perched on the shoulders of Tree. Bird up there blowing a saxophone love song he wished Anna could listen to long enough to hear the African American flavor of his Irish American way of listening to a silent picture show. But, it was Tyrone who told Jackson how to dissect a mistake.

Sometimes one can reach further up the listening chart by understanding the listening limits of a one note song mistake. Sometimes a fleet-foot fox makes more tracks than necessary to create the illusion of a mistake. Sometimes tree rings mistake the jump of leap years. Sometimes an honest mistake is not honest at all.

Tugging on the 14-karat gold necklace that Anna gave him not more than two months after Tyrone introduced her to him, Jackson thought about the difference between love and almost love at first sight. Quietly, Jackson purchased a one-way bus ticket from one life to another. Quietly, he remembered the night of the mistake and smiled to the female ticket lady.

Ursa Minor or Ursa Major

"Debbie Does Dallas" is what the quiet and the unquiet mean girls whispered to the bluebirds and robins perched, so faithlessly, upon the gossip lines that dry spring. April showers must have been waiting for the 1st of May, but the rains decided it was best not to show up until the 1st of June that year.

Deborah Anne Fisher's father took her to the Department of Motor Vehicles during spring break of that year. With no effort at all, she passed the test. She was a legal motor vehicle operator. Sixteen and a half and counting-up to seventeen, she was happy to drive her father's college-professor-looking Volvo home. She was not surprised when he told her that it was now her car. So, there she was, a young lady parking a beige 1975 Volvo station wagon in the Long Horn Cattle High School parking lot.

From then on, she was a constellation in her own night sky. She meticulously aimed, then snapped a photograph of herself as the girl next door, then as a star in Ursa Minor or Ursa Major. It didn't matter if it were on the far side or the near side of the Milky Way Galaxy as long as when the other high school girls at her school looked up into the night sky, they would see her posing near the ladle handle end of one of the Dippers.

Her brownish green eyes, her brunette-ish blonde hair, the Irish in her blood that no one ever told her about, and her figure skater's figure refused to get in the way of her ambition and the other girls' attention. Until she decided what she wanted to be, she cruised in that Volvo station wagon, all four windows down. The wind diving into the windows made her hair think she was driving a convertible. Her father wanted her to go to college some distance away and study music. Her mother wanted her to stay close to home and dance on familiar ice. Indecisive cloudy days told her that she didn't know what she wanted. But clear-sky days told her to try to always remember the dance of her younger days when life was improvisational.

So, as the gossip lines of songbirds would have it that dry spring, it was a somewhat sour-sweet approach that Deborah Anne Fisher had to take when she decided what she wanted to do in life. After looking beneath, the sweaty eyelids of that impending summer, the summer before her senior year of high school, she decided not to remember, as best she could, that night when she couldn't tell whether the burning bushes were moving or not.

Shadows of smoke are hard to forgive, but she moved on in the direction of forgetting. With unveiled promises in her purse, shopping for senior year school clothes as early as late spring was grander, more exciting, and more expensive than the anticipation of sophomore and junior year had ever been. The hot Texas sun moved across the sky, from right to left, as if it cared how hot it would eventually get. Ice cream trucks and young kids provided a soundtrack of summer songs. Things were all right until something reminded her of how dark the shadows were that night. No one would dare mention "Debbie Does Dallas" by its real name.

A slew of Deborah Anne Fisher's relatives on her mother's side were world famous in the neighborhood for having mouths like telegraph stations. Deborah had heard, all of her life that, "People talk and people will talk and some people talk just to be talking," but she paid little attention to the "talk" until the circles of talk among the quiet and unquiet mean girls centered on her. Still, she tried to hold on to what she knew. She knew from an early age that gossip lines, unlike telephone lines, have little desire to follow roadways and railroad tracks into the hearts of cities. The gossip lines she watched her mother's relatives worship seemed to want to follow flight plans airplanes dare not fly. "Talk is cheap," so too many people talk nonstop because they cannot afford to stop talking. She remembered then as clearly as she would remember many years later.

"Debbie Does Dallas." She had one guess, and she guessed the meaning she wanted it to mean. She got the answer wrong. The quiet and unquiet mean girls were talking about her. This was not so much of a revelation as it was a construction-on-the-road detour. Follow the arrows and you will end up where you are going whether you want to be there or not.

Still, somehow, Deborah Anne Fisher knew that small-town boredom had nothing better to say about her being one of the few of them with plans to attend college after graduation. She had always loved Rice University, she entertained the idea of attending Texas A&M, but her mind was set by her father. Pretty solidly, her father pushed her in the direction of St. Mary's University in San Antonio. Her father more than she wanted to see if she could make the strings of a violin play fiddle music with a Texas country and western slant.

"Jealousy, jealousy, jealousy," she said to no one and everyone in particular, simultaneously. She was sitting crossed legged on her bed, looking into an antique floor length mirror next to an Art Deco dresser decorated with enough bottles of lotions and cremes to cover up the quickness of school day get-ready mornings. "Jealousy, jealousy." She knew that she was such a beautiful girl in the eyes of the quiet and unquiet mean girls. She knew they all wanted to look like her when they looked at themselves in fancy boutique store dressing room mirrors. She knew Mark-Down and On Sale department store mirrors loved those girls equally, but the quiet and unquiet mean girls did not want that kind of love. It was not enough adoration and love for them.

Sitting there in her middle-of-the-bed chair, on the surface, she could care less. But beyond and beneath the surface, mushrooms of memory grew in the dark. That one night, one year before her graduation from Long Horn Cattle High School, became a holiday she would never celebrate with a remembering, kind, smile. The darkest night in her life was fragmented into parts she remembered and parts she couldn't figure out how to remember. As if she wanted to notice, again, how dark it was that night, she decided not to decide. Partly because she didn't know how to and partly because she did.

She loved her mother, especially the way her mother smiled. she loved her father's climbing wall attitude, but didn't care too much for Jesus nailed to a cross on a calendar in her friend Analisa's living room. She loved God, matzah balls and Friday night gefilte fish because she had to love something. Ancient sages, according to her mother, believed that the smell of fish on the Sabbath table would encourage couples to be fruitful. As a kid, she was years from being a good little Jewish girl, but she had always been able to convince parents and people of her goodness. She was good enough to convince the horsehair strings of her violin without intending to do so.

Though she was born, bred, and raised in a far corner of a Texas out-stretch town, Deborah Anne Fisher had never been to Dallas. The closest to Dallas she had ever come was 239 miles away. That was that night nine years ago with a boy named Houston. They were laying, looking up at stars, in the back of a flatbed Ford pickup truck with a broken tailgate. Now, at this point in her life, the color of that ole truck did not matter at all, but it was green for the sake of any conversation she was to ever have about the colors painters choose when there is not enough natural light in a studio room. Anyway, she and a handpicked cowboy were stretched out across that flatbed, questioning the formations of stars. Ursa Major or Ursa Minor?

He wasn't just lying there. He was just laying there thinking about baseball running speed and how long it would take to make it to first base with a girl as beautiful as Deborah. She was thinking about playing her violin on a Nashville star-stage set up on the back of the sky. His name was Houston Austin Davis III. His family's money was long and his Lone Star State story had saved him since he was born. Stretched out on the floor of Houston's flatbed, looking up, Deborah Anne wondered why some stars let you see them naked and other stars prefer not to be seen on certain nights.

No wonder, she has often wondered why. But that didn't keep the quiet and the unquiet mean girls from constructing a high school hallway full of walking rumors. Humiliated for being mesmerized by the eyes of a Texas sky full of stars that one night on a flatbed, Deborah Anne never again wanted to read a story that stops at stoplights and crosswalks to let a gossip train with no right of way go by. The giggles of bluebirds and robins and late spring drowning showers talked *Tender is the Night* into ending as a question mark. Why?

Without acknowledgement, some things are easier to swallow, but, still, just as bitter. Without acknowledgement and with great patience, she took out her violin and played long evenings into midnight. So, the rumors persisted until they died, but they never got buried. The Jewish cemetery in her small Texas town was way too small to, easily, bury certain categories of rumors. "Debbie Does Dallas," a porno playing downtown at a backroom theater near somebody. Deborah Anne never knew any of this, so she made up a story to replace what no one wanted to hear about the Long Horn Cattle High School quarterback and three defensive line boys.

Memories, tight across the last of her teenage years like packing tape, always hard to unpackage. Her best friend back then, Analisa was always in her corner. And Analisa stood up for her when she could, but Analisa was so short, the hallway-talking girls didn't notice when she stood. Maybe they did, but they didn't acknowledge that they noticed anything about

Analisa except the envy of how smart Analisa was and her determination. Analisa moved from Rock Springs, Wyoming to Deborah Anne's small town three summers before graduation. Like Deborah Anne, Analisa was an only child. Analisa wanted to be a trial lawyer. She was on the Long Horn Cattle High School debate team and she pre-clerked two days a week at a local family law firm, Hatman, Hatman and Hatman. Deborah Anne was a principal in the Shakespearian drama club, she took three-times-a-week violin lessons, and she was on the cheer-leading squad. Houston played quarterback for the Long Horn Cattle High School Rambling Herd. He escorted three different Homecoming Queens three years in a row. Deborah Anne Fisher was number two.

The early days were good before, Deborah Anne hid, then lost her school spirit for good. And it was for the good, she thinks back, "All my cheers were out of sync and the characters I played, played me more than I played them." She quit everything the year she graduated with honors and disgrace.

That was nine years and two near marriages ago. She never figured out how to walk straight down a wedding bell aisle wearing tall white shoes. Still, she wonders what kind of wedding dress she might have worn if Ursa Minor or Ursa Major had agreed to walk down the aisle with her. She knows she has always loved wedding gifts, but she wonders what style of 24 pcs vintage sterling silver flatware would she now be in possession of and how she would decorate the perfect baby's room.

When she was in her quick-moving tomboy stage, her father would take her fishing, but she never learned how to reel them in, at least ones big enough to keep. She was a master at hooking "throw backs." Maybe, she surmised, that's why the near marriages never got close enough to the alter to matter. Her father died seven years ago, and four years ago her mother remarried a gambler that looked a lot like Kenny Rodgers. That country music-looking fellow lost everything Deborah Anne would have inherited in thirteen months. Then he went back out on the road to sing "Looking for Love in All the Wrong Places" songs deep into the romancing eyes of another sad, single, upper-class, upper middle-aged lady waiting for the sun to come up again before it sets down for good in the quiet years of a comfortable place.

After graduating with a BA in Music, Deborah Anne moved to Waco, as far away from those dark night years as she had ever been. She has been in the same job for the last four years. Eight to five at an accountancy firm, making numbers add up, added up some things for Deborah Anne. Before that, she worked at a frame shop making beautiful frames to mostly match decor and color of the room art. She volunteers at the local community theater, plays a part every now and then to keep theatrics of her life on stages off-Broadway.

Lately, she has been playing her violin more and more. She just loves the untangling sounds of horsehair strings. She smiles often, gracing the face of her freshly tuned Stradivarius. Both of her near-marriages were to soldiers, she wonders why. Maybe dark night memories need fortification to keep from spilling while being carried to wherever one decides to take them. Maybe she thought a soldier could erase black night indelible ink by proposing to wear Marine Dress Blues instead of a tuxedo to the altar. But then again, maybe cowboys and soldier boys are all just boys playing quarterback, playing war games on fields of winning opportunity. It didn't take long for her to think; I'll just leave it at that.

She never could figure out exactly why Houston picked the darkest angle to enter from. She has never been able to say what happened in articulatable terms. But something did happen. At that moment, she loved Houston. He told her he loved her enough times to make it true. The other boys had girlfriends, she thought. The night was too dark to tell if that was true.

A dark foggy blur of boys or the fainting sounds of a herd of something ugly emerged from the dark that night. Recognizable, a question. Quiet as thunder in vacuums of rain, the cowboy shadows came dancing upon the naked music of Houston's car, but the naked ear could not hear above the low hum of car radio speakers. Blinded by the no-light, no moon of the moment, she couldn't figure out how flat a flatbed was supposed to be when the bottom is too dark to see. She couldn't figure out why when they touched her, she didn't feel the heat of star lights. And if she could not feel the heat, if she couldn't remember if they touched her or not, isn't it like they never touched her at all. Memory has the right to edit if memory wants to. All these years, she has left it at that.

Still, she wonders why she so clearly remembers that she had to put her mind elsewhere that night. Somewhere drowning deep, under her breath, talking in her sleep, Deborah Anne Fisher remembers asking Deborah Anne Fisher a simple question, "If the Mississippi River decides to move to Texas, would the bras that cover her bridges need to go up at least a couple of cup sizes to fit beneath the skies in Texas?"

On clear nights, Ursa Minor and Ursa Major had always been brighter and bigger in the life of Deborah Anne. That was until that night and for years afterward. But now... then suddenly and lately, nights decided to be clear. At 27, it did not matter which one of them shone down upon her when she looked up into the night for answers. No question was too big for Deborah Anne, as long as a major or a minor answered.

One day in the life of Deborah Anne, the answer pointed toward a little yellow house on the corner, her favorite coffee shop. There, she watched him put two creams in his coffee enough times to know his history. She noticed the color of his socks to the point that she knew he changed them every day. The way he tied his necktie told her he was an important voice at the meeting room table.

Around the corner at the laundry mat, she watched him fold his clothes enough time to know his personality. She knew he lived alone. It was evident in the size of the wash load and the non-divide of colors. The exact number of quarters to dry his half full clothes basket told her he respected the distance between major and minor piano scales.

Up the street at the neighborhood produce stand, she watched him select herbs enough times to know the culinary measurements of his expressions. She noticed he loved to cook just as she noticed that he didn't like cooking for one and eating alone.

In places noticeable and places not so, she noticed him staring at her enough times to know that he knew her story well enough to recite it with his heart. Her heart knew that he knew that she had never fallen this far beyond *half falling in love* before.

From *Looking for Jack Kerouac*
Winner of the 7th Annual Jack Kerouac International Prize

After Allyson

After Allyson

I'm riding backwards into Chicago. Facing East, I'm sitting in an orange chair at the front end of the viewing car. The Lake Shore Limited is slowing into the city. Hancock, Sears and Mr. Roebuck loom west in the skyline. People are already standing in the aisle, children with their team jackets and baseball caps come alive, the sweet feeling of anticipation filters the lag from slow moving train stale air. Movement makes up its mind and crowds at the exit. With a jolt, the Lake Shore Limited stops.

As an aftershock on a scale equal to a quake on the Richter, I notice her. I notice green. I notice eyes. I notice one long, silent glance and then it's gone, but it comes back. Is she looking at me or is she looking at Mr. Jones, the imaginary jazz and blues man who travels everywhere with me? Does she see me, slow growing dreadlocks, slow turning auburn at the tips of hair growing science? Does she see me sitting here in this orange chair, wearing poet's shoes? Is Irish green the color of eyes? Is quiet anticipation a mistake I need to make? Do I ask too many questions? I don't know.

"There are no mistakes in the tango. If you get tangled up, you just tango on," is a line from *Scent of a Woman*, a movie I once watched alone. *The Last Tango in Paris* is somewhat of a foreign movie starring Marlon Brando I used to know. A compelling depiction of the complications of love, I think, as I make my way from orange chair to green tangle.

She's at Baggage Claim when I arrive. She smiles. Conveyor belts start to turn, luggage starts to push against other luggage, children stare at other children, the soft unsweet voice of loudspeakers announce arrivals and destinations: Albany, Boston, Buffalo, Toronto. Though I'm not leaving until Wednesday at noon, I wait to hear the name of my city called.

Another long glance (my chance) more solid this time, but still silent. She's carrying a violin case. She claims a duffle bag with large blue letters that spell out McALLISTER followed by a smaller lettered social security number. Is that her name or is it some wayward soldier's homecoming hurrah? I don't ask. I claim my Jack Kerouac backpack, stow it away in the train station wall locker, then walk into my first Chicago evening, looking for a place to collect, a place to smoke, a place that doesn't mind neither or either. It's the middle of June in the year of my Lord, 1995. The lake-effect breeze seems, quite easily, to be smiling at flag poles and pigeons.

She's there already, on a bench outside the station, smoking Marlboro Reds, drinking a Diet Coke, and reading city flyers. "You were on my train," I say as I approach her bench situated at the edge of a green tangle. She stares softly and says, "Why is it your train? Perhaps it's mine. I paid my share. And good evening to you my dear Sir."

"Hi," I say as I try to catch up with my equilibrium. She smiles, I smile, she invites me to sit with her for a while in the aisles of shaky anticipation.

"My name is Allyson." "I'm Hudson," I hear myself say, "Hudson Walter Rivers."

The questions of the evening are like the catches of the day. They should be fresh, just taken from water. They should not be presented or eaten too early. So, for the most part, we skip fishing opportunities. We smoke, we talk, but mostly we stare. I am looking at this woman's lipstick look. I stare at periscope tango; she stares at taxi cabs always pulling up and buses always pulling out and police cars that do not move at all. I stare at street signs and Don't Walk lights, at passengers coming and going, at skateboard children playing in the streets of every city in America.

Two strangers on a bench in the evening, a small ten minutes, fifteen minutes, twenty minutes conversation without any inquiry is probably a phenomenal feat.

Finally, I ask, "Where are you headed?" not really wanting to know the answer. What I really want to know is who is this Allyson and why is she so willing to be in this photograph with me, so unwilling to be cropped out of this Chicago Cub evening.

"To a place just south of Joliet, Illinois, called Wilmington," she says. "Ever heard of it?"

"No," I say, "but I'm from Wilmington, North Carolina. Ever hear of that?"

"No," she smiles. "Most people have not," I say as I look away from her green eyes.

"Michael Jordan is from Wilmington," I proudly proclaim.

"So, there you have it," she answers sarcastically. "Hudson Rivers from Wilmington, North Carolina," she announces. "What do you do out there beneath that blue Carolina sky?"

"Well, I don't live there now, I teach liberal arts at a college in Tennessee."

"Beat Alabama, Alabama, the home of the fuckin' 'Tide,'" she sneers as she speaks.

"I'm from Arkansas," she continues, "and I hate hogs, pigs, pig skins, and football. So, what brings the Mr. Professor Rivers to Chi-town?" the inquiry continues.

"I'm on the road. I'm writing a book. I'm looking for Jack Kerouac," I say.

"A book? Tell me about it," she smiles.

"Well," I start, "Jack Kerouac was..."

"No," she interrupts, "let me tell you about me first. That way, if you're boring, I can just leave. You'll know who I am, and

I won't know who you are. I'll leave with what I came with, and you will leave with me."

Puzzled as I am, I say, "That would be good."

So, I stop staring and talking and start to listen, but the entangling green comes to get me and before I know it, I'm noticing Allyson again. I'm noticing her hair, wild, uncombed, trying not to be blonde, her face casual but not too round, her ears pulled slightly to the weight of rings, her teeth, her grin, her skin, her chin, her lashes, her brows, her lips, and her lipstick look.

If one gets locked in, five seconds can seem like a five minute stretched-out wait. I'm catching only the ends of Allyson's sentences. I re-adjust myself on my end of the bench and try to hear words from a pretty mouth. She tells me about New Orleans and how she had to leave, about Little Rock and how she had to leave. "Now, I'm in Chicago," she says, "My father is from these parts. Twenty-six years ago, he lived right here in downtown Chicago in a lake front place. For whatever reason, my father had to leave. He moved from Chicago to Little Rock. I'm moving from Little Rock to Chicago. We get along. I love my Daddy, but we don't talk much at all. When I was a little girl, my father was the hero and the stranger. Mama, bless her soul, would run him off. He always came back until that one time. Mama said, she was a pretty girl. Mama said, she looked about first-year-in-college age. Mama is always telling people's ages without using numbers. She's odd that way. When Daddy left, I was seventeen. He must have been, let's see, maybe 39. Mama met Daddy after he'd lived in Little Rock for a year. They were married by the end of his second year. According to Mama, I took my first steps on the day of their first anniversary. Ever since Daddy first started going away, Mama has had two boyfriends, Mr. Ralph and Johnny Ray. She thinks I don't know, but I know she knows I know. I always tease her 'bout how her Johnny Ray can't sing."

"Tomorrow morning early, I'll be leaving for Just South of Joliet as my father calls it. I'll be staying with Daddy's sister, Aunt Pearl. I've never seen Aunt Pearl. Of course, I've spoken to her over the phone plenty of times, even used to write to her when I was a kid and needed donations and contributions for some school-sponsored function. He always said he would, but Daddy never took us to visit his family up North. I mean, we do have family there on Mama's side, and Mama has met her in-laws, and I've seen my grandparents a number of times in a number of places, joint two-day vacations and such. Yeah, we have family in Little Rock, a whole clan of nothing but good country people yelling 'Go Hogs.' I had to leave. I went to New Orleans to study music, but the music studied me more than I studied the music. I needed a change, so I got a bus ticket, threw it away, and walked onto the train. Nobody never said nothing."

"Where's your father now?" I ask.

"Oh, he's somewhere on the outskirts of Salt Lake City, living with his Mrs. Prettier and Mrs. Younger wife," Allyson answers as if she is answering an essay exam question.

"Really!" I say, "I'm headed to Salt Lake City in a few days."

"Well, bless the Father, bless the Son, and The Mormon Tabernacle Choir," Allyson says, "and kiss my Daddy for me. Tell him I love him, but I don't like him very much anymore."

Allyson half-smiles and continues to tell the family story from the only side she knows. As she talks, I think, "I didn't ask for all of this." Cigarette after cigarette continues to burn into the conversation. Silence puts them out at the very end of each last long drag.

"Aunt Pearl is a sweet woman according to Mama," Allyson

talks as she continues to drink Diet Coke from a can. Mr. Jones is drinking another can of Old Milwaukee while he hums, softly, a saxophone song.

"Mama said when they were young, they met at a wedding in Cedar Rapids of all places. In my twenty-two years, I've spoken to her a lot, especially when I was a kid. You know, when you are a kid and your mother puts you on the phone? 'Now you go in there and say hello to your Daddy's sister.' Then she would tail it off with some kind of guilt trip,... 'cause your Daddy ain't here to speak with his sister.' So, that's my acquaintance with Daddy's sister, and now I'm going Just South of Joliet to live with her, until, as they say, 'I save some money, get my own place,' here in Chi-Town."

"I'm not exactly sure where I'm going. I only know where I came from," I tell Allyson. "Ten days ago, I was in Rocky Mount, North Carolina, searching for Kerouac's Buddha pine forest, trying to look out for snakes and ticks. Before that, I hitchhiked from Chattanooga to Atlanta. I got one ride. A young drunk white kid took me all the way to the steps of the train station. The next day, I got off the train in Durham, North Carolina, rented this European blue minivan, and rode until I found Buddha's Place located exactly across the highway from where Kerouac's sister, Nin, lived in Rocky Mount. So where am I headed? I don't know. I know what my itinerary says. I know I'm on the road, and I know I'm looking for Jack Kerouac. As I rode in, the sign did not WELCOME or UNWELCOME me to Chicago. I kinda really just don't know."

"Oh, Hudson, you're so philosophical," Allyson says.

"And so are you," I say.

Allyson has read *On the Road*. She starts to talk about the beatniks and the now generation X YZ.

"I liked Sal," Allyson says. With delight and anticipation, I listen, thinking, "This woman may be able to help me find Jack Kerouac tonight."

"Allison's smile is warm and fixed. Her shoulders are square, soft, and silent. Allyson's jewelry is all silver and slightly tarnished. Allyson has been on the road a long time, though she tells me, she left New Orleans less than a week ago.

"I went to The City first to visit friends," she says. "I don't like New York. Too many ways to get lost, too many places to go, too many people who don't smile, too many taxi cabs and buses and sirens, too many numbers instead of names for streets, too many things to steal from oneself." As she talks, her crescent moon earrings swing against the sides of her thin white face and softly come to rest against the edge of her slender white neck. Allyson is as white as any white girl I've ever seen, but she's not ghostly. Allyson is Black Irish white.

Allyson is not beautiful like the cover of some magazine. She is not the All American Girl who happens to live next door. Allyson has never been a jump-up-and-down cheerleader for her small-Little-Rock-town-Friday-night football team. Allyson does not care who wins what or what wins who. Allyson just doesn't care. Allyson talks. I stare as the wind off the lake partly unwraps Allyson's wrap-around skirt, revealing legs.

Allyson is not glamorous. Allyson is plain and pretty like the edges of the Midwest. No made-up face, no make-up story, just a red lipstick look for Allyson.

"Tom Petty and the Heartbreakers," I'd say if I had to guess the music that makes Allyson. I feel like breaking somebody's heart, but this evening I'm a long way from love. I'm in Chicago, it's windy, it's 7:15 Central Standard Time, and I haven't had a shower in three days. Wish I could wash my face in a friendly sink. I think I want to stop thinking for a while. Tonight, I want to listen completely to Allyson.

Allyson's fingers are long and thin and soft to the tiniest of my touch like taking a light as she holds her Zippo for me. Each cigarette takes a bit longer to catch a hold of Allyson's flame. Her hands are the hands of an artist. One finger painted red half across a single nail on either. Her clothes are the clothes of one who models nude for an artist. Everything is larger and longer than life like some kind of personified Andy Warhol painting.

Allyson's boots are perfect cowboys, seven and one-half medium. I know, because as a youngster, I worked as a salesclerk at an all-day-Saturday-afternoon women's shoe store. I've seen my share of sizes and I've seen my share of Allysons, but none of them look like this Allyson. Allyson's boots are red, made from the skin of a red alligator, I suppose. A rare gator, probably, found in the swamps outside Baton Rouge.

Nearly everyone passing notices the color of Allyson's boots. The ones who do not notice, notice the color of our faces with not-so-short-disapproving interracial stares. Interracial, I hate that word. Everybody is interracial and if you are not, then you need to be inter-something. Intercalary, intercultural, inter-disciplinary, interglacial, intergalactic or just plain and simply interunderstanding. I don't know about you Mr. and Mrs. Walk-by-look-left-on-a-sly, but I'm starting to get into the international contours and curves of red alligator boots.

Allyson's body is built like that of a young goddess. Everything builds upon the science of mythology, shoulders, arms, breasts, and butt. Everything but Allyson's legs. Her legs should be on one of those panty hose television commercials with ZZ Top and the Texas Cornroosters singing that satisfaction song in the background.

Allyson's legs, if I were to write it down, would take up a whole page of description before I could get part way down to her butterfly three-colored tattoo. When Allyson crosses her legs, I have to uncross mine. When Allyson stands, I sit. Long legs, designer legs, Juliet Prowse legs. What would Allyson look like in a pair of Gloria Vanderbilt's? Angels must have legs like Allyson. But you can't pay too close attention to what I say, I've been riding on the train too many nights in a row. I don't know. Legs in this mirror may not be as long as they appear. Mr. Jones has switched his brand of beer and wandered off course with a big ass, black blues woman. I don't know if I will see him again, for a while.

Allyson's face is built to get away with almost anything Allyson chooses. A sweet face with sweet lines that curve into the natural shadow around her eyes as the green is drawn out like a blue shadow pencil. Allyson's morning face does not need to be touched by anything except a red-orange lipstick look. Allyson's face has always been able to talk smoothly through any place.

Allyson and I, sitting on this bench. For how long? I cannot rightly say. Twenty minutes, forty minutes? It's hard to guess at the passage of time when you ride on the train too many days in a row. All you know about is distances and differences. Each town is a certain distance from the next and each city looks at you differently, treats you differently, and eats you completely up, differently.

When one takes a course in geography, one learns to read the city by walking streets. The city consumes the geography student more slowly. The city sometimes enjoys the geographer's company. Sometimes it's delicious. I guess, if you chew long enough. Everything tastes like chicken when taste buds and train station vending machines marry. But tonight is a delicious night, home fried and golden brown, along the streets of Lake Michigan Place.

"Hudson," Allyson turns to face me, "You know what?"

"What is it, Allyson?"

"We're sitting here watching the Chicago skyline from the inside out," she says, looking up. "It makes sense, Hudson. The city grows from the inside out. Chicago probably started out as a general store. In 1871 somebody (I think they blamed it on a cow) burned down Chicago and we're sitting here tonight landscaping the skyline, admiring the beauty of the rebuilt." Allyson rolls on, talking about Carl Sandburg, The Chicago poet, and how he loved the scope of Illinois land.

"Gwendolyn Brooks followed Sandburg's steps," I say. "In 1950, when Gwen won the Pulitzer for *Annie Allen*, the awarding committee did not know she was Negro until the press called one afternoon and that's when the atom bomb was dropped into the center of the literary canon. According to the sparks, July 4th came early that year. 'Oh say... was too blind to see'"

Allyson listens, sitting perfectly still except for drags of smoke. Suspended animation. I continue to talk until I lose my point like a golf ball that misses the green, sand trapped.

"Hudson," Allyson hesitates in that space that determines Hudson as a statement from Hudson as a question mark.

The wind is starting to pick up again. Allyson's skirt is starting to realize, I'm sitting to Allyson's immediate left.

"Lake Michigan town is way cool tonight," Allyson says,

"When I was a real little girl, I loved going to town. Every Saturday morning, Daddy would pack us up in his always new, always Ford pick-up truck, and we would hit the road. Twenty miles outside of Little Rock, such a short distance as I look back, but you know what, Hudson? Twenty miles in Arkansas was a long way back then. That was when Mama and Daddy were happy, when they enjoyed being Mr. and Mrs. Lower Middle Class America, walking the streets of Little Rock. On either side of me, each would take a hold of my hand. I remember skipping along, golden brownish locks cascading to the wind. Some days I would ride a drugstore pony."

Allyson is a talker. She talks too much about too many different things, but that's fine. I need to hear the same woman's voice for long periods of time.

Everything revolves around Allyson. And I, quite the happy one, sane, insane, hungry, dazed, drugged, drunk, confused, and in love with a woman I've not seen in a long time. Perhaps crazy like Patsy Cline walking after midnight should be added to the list. Yet I, quite the happy one, hanging out with Allyson.

Well, something leads to another thing and another thing leads to the Just Come In Coffee House. Five blocks up on Canal Street, right on Randolph Street, walk fast past the Wino Gallo, left on State Street. The Just Come In Coffeehouse. Allyson talks all the way.

I pour coffee for each of us from a decorative sterling silver antique pot. A square blue glass burns a blue candle in the middle of a cloth red and white picnic tablecloth. A ceiling fan makes blue candlelight dance like midnight jazz. I light cigarettes for each of us.

"Hudson, tell me about Kerouac."

I look at Allyson. Questions flood into a space I didn't know was there. Why did I wait hours for a ride out of Nashville, North Carolina? Why did I pick up Billy Jack on his way to California, hitchhiking through Chapel Hill? Why did I step across a No Trespass line in Rocky Mount to take a piss in the Buddha Woods? Why have I slept on the train so many nights in a row? Why did I walk from one side of Philadelphia to the other?

"Kerouac kept falling in love with his mother," I say. "Picture this: John Louis Kerouac sitting at his typewriter on the kitchen table in his mother's apartment in Ozone Park. After Kerouac went on the road in '47, he never lived anywhere again. Almost a year after Kerouac's father died, while he was writing *The Town and The City*, he met Neal Cassady for the first time. Neal could tango. He was Marlon Brando and James Dean. Before Brando was Brando, before Dean was Dean, Neal was Neal. Neal was the crazy one. Neal was a nut and Kerouac loved every minute of his life when he was with Neal. Neal made Kerouac laugh. They would laugh from New York City to Salt Lake City, from Chicago to San Francisco. They always stopped in Denver to gas up. They drank tea all the way. They were fucked up on something six and one-half days a week. They did not go to church. Neal could've been an astronaut just as easily as he could've been Harry Houdini. He could've sold cars at a Chevrolet dealership, if he hadn't been a car thief. Neal drove like he lived, wide-fucking-open. One time, Neal drove from San Francisco to pick up Kerouac from his sister Nin's house in Rocky Mount, North Carolina. Before they headed back west, Neal drove Kerouac and his mother to New York and back to Rocky Mount in a day and a half. When Neal had a car, Neal had a Hudson. When Neal didn't have a car, Neal trusted the first one he could find locked or unlocked. One year, while they were in Denver, Neal stole thirty cars and Kerouac rode shotgun in every one of them."

"Why am I telling you about Neal when you asked about Kerouac?"

"Well, yeah," Allyson puzzles for a second.

"Neal was the hero in *On the Road*. Kerouac created his own Neal," I say. "When *On the Road* came out, people started buying it and reading it and reacting to it as if Kerouac had made himself the hero. They started treating Kerouac like he was Dean Moriarty, but Kerouac was Sal Paradise, the guy always in the shadows of things. Neal kept being Neal while Kerouac became another Neal in the minds of many. Many times, Kerouac tried to lose himself by going the mountain, alone at the top. Four months he would stay in fire lookout towers, looking for solitude, space, and smoke. He tried until he lost all sense of direction. He went down into the railroad earth. When he came up, Kerouac was still Neal.

Kerouac wrote, wrote, wrote often using the size of his notebook page for the form and length of the piece. In three long nights, he wrote *The Subterraneans.* Kerouac wrote, wrote, wrote. Truman Capote called it typewriting."

"Oh," Allyson says, "I like Capote."

"I do too," I say, "but Capote didn't care much for Jack Kerouac it seems. Jack was too much jazz." I keep talking partly because I sometimes like hearing myself talk and partly because I had Allyson's undivided and divided attention at the same time. A rare feat. I keep talking, "Kerouac invented the Beat by listening to Bird. He insisted to the media that he alone understood the Beat. When someone tried to pin him down concretely, Kerouac would start talking about Bird being the definition of the Beat."

"Charlie Parker, you mean?" Allyson gestures her question.

"Yeah," I say, "Kerouac's jazz was Bird. In order to meet Kerouac, one has to go through Kerouac's Buddha."

"Stop being a professor, Hudson, and talk like normal people," Allyson jokes.

"I talk like I talk, Allyson, my dear," I say, smiling at her smiling at me over more coffee and more cigarette smoke.

"According to this book I read last summer by Robert George Reisner," I continue, "'Bird's music is so perfect that it's scientific. His music is so structurally perfect that you cannot enlarge a note to make it better. If Bird had been born lucky, he couldn't have played any better.'"

"Bird was an angel," I say, "everything he did was excusable. If Bird cleared $750 a week, he'd be broke the next day. Bird was always broke. He was tricky and he was charming. Bird would get your last dollar. He was always borrowing money and he never paid any of it back." One can tell that I've listened to and am Counting Crows, but I don't tell Allyson about the musical impact of bird and my improvisation.

"The funny thing," I tell Allyson, "Nobody expected it back."

"Bird loved Picasso and Rembrandt. He loved movies, good and bad. He loved women, but his horn came before a woman. He was a conversationalist. He could cook anybody about anything at any time. A lot of people call Bird, Yardbird 'cause Bird love himself some fried chicken.

"Bird was Kerouac's Buddha," Allyson says.

"And Kerouac's was Neal," I say. Allyson smiles.

"Tell me more, tell me more," she grabs my arm like a small kid in a storybook store.

"Bird called everybody baby. That was his tragedy. Everybody loved him to death. 'Bird ain't dead,' is what Charlie Mingus said, 'Bird's hiding out somewhere, and he'll be back with some new shit that will scare everyone else to death.'"

"Miles Davis said, 'When I went to New York to study at Juilliard, I spent my first month's allowance looking for Bird.'"

"Bird loved his mother. He always called her long distance. He loved his children and he loved Chan."

"Who's Chan?" Allyson leans forward with her one half red fingernail playing with the space between her teeth. "Chan, that's a beautiful name," she says.

"Chan was the upper class lady that saved a black Bird for as long as she could."

"Was she white?" Allyson asks.

"Yeah," I say.

"Bird was Kerouac's Buddha. His Buddha was to write like Bird played sax. Some days Kerouac was there. But, in Kerouac's words, you have to remember that jazz is one profession where being white is not an advantage."

Though I often think I don't, I do talk a lot when I get on a merry-go-round. After too many cups of coffee, too many cigarettes, too many hors d'oeuvres, we smile at the break we're taking. Allyson slides her chair close and wraps me like a scarf in Vermont in the wintertime. For a moment I love Allyson. For a moment my lips barely touch the red of Allyson's lipstick look.

Allyson came to Chicago to study music at the Institute. Allyson thinks, up here there are more streets to navigate, more places to turn the boat around.

Allyson's coffee house is an erotic blend with heavy feelings. A place like any other coffee house on State Street, any street, in any town. Same pictures on stucco walls, same rooster warrior painting, pointing at the exit with a spear, same crowded orange and green plastic chair smell.

Allyson's coffee house has a fireplace and shelf of books. There's light FM music and a red magic carpet worn to less than crimson where the same people have sat at the same table way too long, way too many times.

Allyson's coffee house is covered with small and smaller circle conversation with an even mix of men and women, a few Blacks, no Japanese, no Chinese, and no Mexicans. Everybody is the same. The same woman with a woman sitting at the bar. The same man with a man, impeccably dressed at the other end. The same couples are here. You know the ones I mean. The couples that are not supposed to be couples. The ones who sit in plain and clear view, hoping not to be seen together, trying to live out three hours in an hour and a half.

In this room of blended heavy smells, I still smell the whirlwind rooster warrior painting, cocked crooked on a blue stucco wall. As much as he wants us to leave by way of a pointing spear, we sit here listening to coffee drip. Allyson and I are sitting in the seats reserved for the ones who are like us. The ones without regard for the way the wind decides to blow in Chicago tonight.

"Coffee house rooster warriors are all the same," I think as Allyson and I exit the Just Come In Coffee House. Sideways, Mr. Jones exits through the DO NOT ENTER door and sideways he crosses the sidewalk on RED with a beer can pointing away from his mouth towards the sky.

Allyson walks like a cowgirl. She tells me she prefers appaloosas. Allyson likes to walk. She follows her own way. I follow Allyson. The names of street signs glow at night, cars do what cars do on State Street at night, men wearing baseball caps ask for money, couples hold hands, bus riders wait, wait, late night window shoppers take their sweet nighttime. Faint sounds of Chicago blues ease out from every crack in the wall.

Silence is upon us as we walk, a comfortable silence, the kind you sometimes find in silent picture shows. Enlightenment in a very small dose. Kerouac was looking for enlightenment. He looked at Buddha and he looked at Bird. He didn't look in the middle. "Do you think enlightenment can be found in the middle?" I almost ask. Silence is such a beautiful thing. We walk.

"Let's go somewhere and rock-a-while," Alyson says, breaking little tabs of enlightenment into much smaller pieces, a little explosion, a flash in the sky. Fireworks, falling lights shape a willow tree.

"Sure," I say, not knowing to what Allyson is referring. Anything with the word "rock" in it, must be all right. Mick Jagger is older than the President of the United States of America.

Before she finishes asking question number two, I say, "Yes."

"Do you like Stevie Nicks?"

"Well, I know this place," she hops and skips as she speaks. I know this way cool place where Stevie plays live at the Red Rock every night. Everything comes in box sets, and the jazzbox takes dollar bills.

"Way cool," I say, imitating Allyson.

"It's a ways away. We'll have to take a bus or a cabbie," Allyson says.

"Let's take the bus. Oh, Hudson, let's take the bus." "You can write about the night bus people. Make it romantic."

"Way cool," I say.

"Too way cool," Allyson laughs. "Too way cool tonight, Hudson."

"A bus sounds good," I say, thinking. "This woman is the sweetest woman I've ever seen."

Hands holding onto a kite string night, a perfect fit. Swinging arms as we run, jumping puddles together. We know not what angle to follow, so we follow contours of streets past brilliant pink and blue neon lights, past been-closed-for-hours-now hamburger stands and grills, past storefront mannequins posing nude for the moon, past the tourist ghost with his and her Mastercard, Visa, and American Express. The tourist ghosts know not to leave home without them. Past live bands playing LIVE in cellars, past more brilliant neons, lavender this time. Past men wearing baseball caps. The Chicago Cubs and the Chicago White Sox never really do stop playing baseball in Chicago.

Every city is a ghost town with dead office buildings left over from the heydays, buildings that used to be office buildings for important men with important sounding names, names like William Franklin Wright III or perhaps Theodore Jefferson Hoover IV. What about Roosevelt Washington Jr.? Roosevelt Washington Jr. didn't have an office on this now-dead street. Just a shoeshine stand came with his important sounding name. No window office space for Mr. Roosevelt Washington Jr. in the Negro part of where the trash-picking people lived in this Chicago city town.

I look over at Allyson. She's looking out from the other side. I wonder what she sees from her city bus window view. I wonder if Allyson sees Mrs. Minnie Washington Jr. still waiting, waiting at the very end of a very long line, waiting, waiting at a bus stop somewhere because the Mister retired after forty years without a golf cart. I wonder if Allyson sees Mrs. Minnie Washington still riding this same bus in the daytime, making the early shift, going to clean the homes of Mrs. Hoover and Mrs. Wright. I wonder as Allyson reaches up to snap the cord.

"We'll disembark here, Hudson, my Lord."

"Disembark it is my lady," I say as we step down into the laughing streets. The city is alive again. It's a good time to tango in Chicago. It's one o'clock in the morning Central Standard Time.

The Just Come In Gay Club is Allyson's club. Allyson's club is situated on the edge of the tall building district on LaSalle Street. Admission is free. No membership required. Drinks are expensive. All the patrons are men except for Allyson. This place is wide open space that used to be a disco room with flashing lights, mirrors full of people reflecting spinning disco balls and designer jeans. Now the lights are always low, a single beam outlines the dance floor. The jazz box waits for Allyson. Mr. Jones don't want to hear no gay-club-techno-rock, but they sell beer, he is here, sideways.

Four plays for a one dollar bill in a CD money changer, we play eight and dance straight into the ceiling of abstract design. It feels like Stevie is singing on everybody's radio at the same time. A-4 is *Sister Honey* and Stevie is enchanting in her dance. "Don't let that golden hair get in your way, baby," is a refrain. G-20 is *Gypsy*, and C-23 is *The Highwayman*. That's me and Jack Kerouac and Mr. Jones.

We dance close and we dance apart. When we dance close, I feel the points in Allyson's shirt. When we dance apart, I see them.

"Hudson," Allyson whispers as softly as Marilyn Monroe calling up Jack Kennedy at one o'clock in the morning. "Miss White House operator, let me speak to the President," She knows Jackie is in Brazil on a goodwill mission.

"Yes, Allyson," I respond from a dance daze.

"I want to play music that will make people dance," she says, "I don't think people dance enough, I really don't."

"Black people dance," I say, "sometimes all we can do is dance."

"But dancing is good, Hudson, yes?"

"You're right," I say.

"I like dancing with you Hudson," She pushes away to study my face, my red-black Masai warrior's face I look into green and fade into rhythms of this dancing room floor. Too quickly upon us is the last song. We dance slowly, moving without moving, hands stretching into arms into fingertips, stretching into air. Our bodies, wet, sway softly, almost no movement. Then the movement comes in small circles that enlarge, concentric. We dance like the Welch Witch, herself, Live at the Red Rock Amphitheater.

We rock. We rock. We rock until the walls come down. And Stevie is here masquerading in long flowing white air. I'm here, but Allyson is everywhere.

"Hudson, you know what?" Allyson takes both my hands into hers, "You know what?" she says.

"What?" "What will we do next?" Anticipating the question, I step in front of Allyson.

"Tonight, where will we sleep?" she asks.

The question of the night surfaces like another catch of the day, but somehow it seems so unimportant.

"I don't know. Where would you like to sleep?" I ask.

Before she answers, I say, "Sleep, sleep who wants to sleep." The night is still a baby that needs to be fed. Let's take a cabbie somewhere, anywhere. We could go to the airport and pretend we are flying out to Barcelona, or we could pretend we just flew in from the South of France and immediately take a cabbie back downtown. We could go to London or Ireland and play in the fog."

"Or to Tanzania and ride zebras." Allyson says.

"Yes Allyson, zebras. Zebras I love."

I think of a walk in my neighborhood early one summer evening. I stopped to watch children play. Two little black girls and a little white boy. Some things are black and white I thought as I walked away.

"Some things are black and white," I say.

"Yeah! zebras," Allyson laughs,

"Let's be zebras tonight, Hudson, tonight we'll sleep together in the train station."

"We'll surprise the keepers of the zoo," I say.

"Zookeepers, zookeepers. Who cares about them. Tonight is a circus, Hudson, the greatest show on earth and we are at the very top of a farrago wheel. Tonight is your night. When I claim my fiddle, I'll play for you, Hudson."

"From zebras to farrago wheel to fiddle," I think.

Bartenders are zookeepers. Train stations are always waiting. People are always going somewhere.

"Let's go," Allyson says.

Five dollars for a flat, bumpy ride, one dollar for a tip to a cabbie man who does not tip his hat to Allyson, who does not know Mr. Jones is riding shotgun, who does not say a word that doesn't need to be said. "Union Station," he announces in a curved Cuban voice.

It's almost three o'clock when we finally sit down on our bench. Allyson's arm is around my shoulders. We breathe deeply. Allyson had to pee. Allyson had to get her luggage, I had to get mine. Allyson wanted a Diet Coke. We both needed cigarettes.

"I really love Stevie Nicks," I say.

"You love everybody," Allyson says "and everybody loves you. You call everybody Darling and everybody calls you Darling too." "Ever hear that song by KT Oslin?" she asks.

"I know the song," I say, "I like KT."

"But you love Stevie."

"Yeah," I say, "I love Stevie.

As I contemplate the direction of the wind, Allyson unzips her fiddle case and starts to tune the skyline over Chicago to a nice, cool, hours after midnight breeze.

"Has anyone ever written anything for you?" she asks without looking away from fiddle strings.

I think about how to answer, but I do not say anything, thinking how often silence contains the only answer. She continues, "You know, writers are always writing books and poems and plays and stories for the world to read. They are always writing children's stories for children, always writing for the infamous and famous. Writers write to the world, but the world does not write back. It's sad how the unnamed almost never gets named without some kind of tragedy. Do you know what I mean, Hudson?"

I smile, 'Yes, Allyson."

"Hudson," she says, "Look at me! I wrote something for you."

Amazement starts to enter my mind, but I am not amazed at what she says or what she does anymore. I look at Allyson. Mr. Jones looks into an empty cooler.

"You know, it's interesting," she says, "how the world turns when you don't watch soap operas, when you don't know who Erica Kane is and you don't care how many times she has been married, when you don't know what time *General Hospital* comes on, when you don't care about time slots and ratings. For a year I was lost in a world of opera music and men, most of whom I didn't like very much. I was living on the skirts of the Quarter. I was a different Mardi Gras woman every day. One night after I started sleeping alone, I had this dream, a dream about flowers, orange red flowers, a tulip field in Amsterdam. And there I was playing my fiddle in the center of a photograph. I was playing for a picture taker I could not see. The picture taker man was you, Hudson. I know now. I didn't know your name, but I knew I would find you here in Windytown. Chicago is your town. You like wind. In my dream I was Dutch with hair as yellow as Van Gogh's. I was in Amsterdam, but the wind that moved the tulips was blowing in from Chicago. This is my town too, Hudson. Windytown is not just for the two of us, it's for all of us who blow across this land like tumbleweed looking for the things we cannot find. I'm looking for a crowded silver stage upon which I wish to play fiddle music. You're looking for Jack Kerouac. We found each other in Windytown. You'll find Kerouac and I'll find a stage. It may not be crowded and it may not be silver, but I'll play fiddle music anyway. Thanks for telling me about Bird and about Sal and Dean."

"Sal and Dean were Butch and Sundance," I say, "and Bird was Bird."

"They were chasing the same wind we now chase," Allyson says.

"They couldn't catch it and we can't either, Hudson."

"Have you ever seen a field full of tulips on a windy day?"

"I have," Allyson says. "It's the most beautiful thing in the whole wide world. It doesn't take your breath. It gives. It gives voice to the breeze."

Allyson poses the perfect fiddle pose, turns to look directly into my eyes, and says, "There I was playing fiddle in a field of orange-red tulips. The sun was bright in Amsterdam that day. The sky was Van Gogh blue. Some photographs are too beautiful to take."

"One day not long after my dream," Allyson continues, "I was walking as I often do in the afternoon. I came upon a flower shop, one that I'd not seen. It was a small shop, probably been there for years. I walked in, walked to the flower shop case, opened the door, and took out a single orange-red tulip. I walked straight out. Nobody never said nothing."

"At home I put it in a simple white vase. After three days, I dried it flat in a book. It was an ordinary book then. Now I know. It's the collected poems of Paul Goodman called *The Lordly Hudson*."

I stare at Allyson. I don't know what to say. What could I say? I don't say anything.

Into the distance of the morning sky, I look for my star. I do not make a wish. This moment I have everything I need. Allyson stands ready to play.

"There is no title for this song," she says "*Hudson*, we'll call it for now It's about this river and this young girl who falls in love with the sound of water." Allyson plays. A man across the street stops to listen. A woman waiting on a taxi breaks the red heel of a red tall shoe. A night flight into O'Hare stops in midair. The control tower does not understand, but listens so intently, anyway.

Inside is a different world. Union Station is lit up like a train station. A few people going somewhere, looking for something. Other people going anywhere, looking for anything. Single mothers dragging single children from one train to the station to another train. Little Susie and Little Derrick with thumbs in their mouths drag teddy bears. Little Johnny is not screaming and running tonight. He's asleep on his single mother's lap. Little Lisa is also asleep in her single mother's arms. But Little Bo Peep, bless his little soul, is wide awake, twirling his hair, watching us as we watch him and his single mom look for an uncrowded space in an uncrowded train station. The ticket agent watches us, the men wearing baseball caps watch us, college girls and boys with backpacks and Birkenstocks watch us, a brother with a huge Angela Davis afro watches us.

"Over there is where we'll sleep," Allyson orders like a drive-through window. "Two large fries, a double veggie-burger with twice the cheese and a small diet coke."

"That will be $5.17 out a $6… 83 cents will be your change."

"Keep it," I say, "I don't need it tonight."

An unzipped sleeping bag fits perfectly into any corner. Allyson's blanket quickly follows and covers us. We snuggle into a silver decorative baby spoon. We sleep.

Morning is another story. Where is Allyson? What time is it? Her bus is gone? Maybe not. Did she leave a note? I don't see no note!

"Sir, what time do you have?" a voice from nowhere and everywhere, confused as simple confusion.

I wake to the smell of patchouli. Her blanket hugs me. The side she slept on reaches for me, warm.

"Good morning to Allyson," I say. Questions roll in as I roll up.

Did I leave my finger prints at the scene? Did I touch her beyond the warmth of kind and gentle human touch? I do not know. If I did and do not remember, did Chicago burn again? Did I say to her everything I wanted to whisper in my sleep? I do not know.

It's time to go. I fold and unfold blanket and sleeping bag twice each because I'm thinking in repetition. Two memories collide and become one that's even more difficult to discern. My Kerouac backpack adds to the beauty of her blanket well. Mr. Jones has a blank stare glued but only to edges of his hard, blue, unwashed face. In the train station men's room there is always a train station mirror. As a planted red "Good morning my Hudson," kiss on my forehead, Allyson's magic is in this mirror. I stare at myself for longer than I can bear to look into the face of this world.

Her address, why didn't I get it? Her long-distance phone number is not in my book. Just a red lipstick look planted early on a sleeping, smooth, dark, morning, train station, unwashed face.

Was she too good to be true or was she too true to be good for me, herself, the world? Was she an angel? I do not know. "There are no mistakes in the tango, you get tangled up, you just tango on." It's 8:15 in Chicago, and the wind is blowing again, in from the east. I exit and face west.

The two people sitting on our bench now, now figure wind velocity on a Chicago city map. Pigeons check to see if the two people are having velocity for breakfast. People get off buses, before they walk past the velocity of the two people. Cabbies shuffle for position-velocity directly in front of the two people. A baseball cap man velocities it all from the other side of a no-way stop street. Moment and decision meet. I smile.

I'm walking, now, into the arms of a green summer morning beneath a spiritual blue sky, thinking, "Jack Kerouac will be easier to find now, after Allyson."

About the Author

Earl S. Braggs is the author of 14 books of poetry and a memoir, *A Boy Named Boy.* His website is earlsbraggs.com

www.ingramcontent.com/pod-product-compliance
Lightning Source LLC
LaVergne TN
LVHW030921080826
845145LV00013B/3002

* 9 7 8 1 9 6 3 6 9 5 4 7 2 *